BROG the STOOP

From the corner of his eye, Brog saw Redeye moving to the attack, and he put in a burst of speed. Redeye gave a roar, fearing that his victim was about to escape him, and changed the angle of his charge in an effort to cut him off.

"Faster, Brog, faster!" urged Pik.

Brog's long legs were covering the ground at a tremendous pace, and it was touch and go whether he reached the trees before, or at the same time as Redeye.

A figure hurtled past Brog from out of the bushes, too fast for him to see who it was, but he heard the roar of surprise from Redeye, and the thud of bodies behind him before he was grabbed by Pik, and dragged, still running, into the thickness of the Treelands.

BROG THE STOOP

Joe Boyle

Cover illustration by Brian Froud

SCHOLASTIC

Scholastic Children's Books,
Scholastic Publications Ltd,
7–9 Pratt Street, London NW1 0AE, UK

Scholastic Inc.,
730 Broadway, New York, NY 10003, USA

Scholastic Canada Ltd,
123 Newkirk Road, Richmond Hill,
Ontario, Canada L4C 3G5

Ashton Scholastic Pty Ltd,
P O Box 579, Gosford, New South Wales,
Australia

Ashton Scholastic Ltd,
Private Bag 1, Penrose, Auckland,
New Zealand

First published by Scholastic Publications Ltd, 1993

Text copyright © Joe Boyle, 1993
Cover illustration copyright © Brian Froud, 1993

ISBN 0 590 55430 1

Typeset by TW Typesetting, Midsomer Norton, Avon
Printed by Cox & Wyman Ltd, Reading, Berks

10 9 8 7 6 5 4 3 2 1

For Lesley, the light of my life

CHAPTER 1

The mists hung thin over the tangled tree roots and vines, and the damp air caused the tree bark to glisten and trickle.

All was still.

From the distance came the low, hollow growl of a hungry Gork, as he lumbered through the Darkness, and the sound echoed eerily across the whole of Drabwurld.

In the dry, warm hollow beneath the great Magnatree, Brog the Stoop heard the sound through the haze of his sleep, and he settled closer to the warm, furry body of his mother, Blid. Patiently, as she had done each and every Blacktime of her adult life, Blid sat and waited for the Blackhours to slip away, one great, furry arm curled protectively around her little one, the other paw gently stroking his head as she rocked rhythmically backwards and forwards.

Her huge eyes, now at their largest in the Blacktime, misted with memory as she thought back over the events of the last two Moonruns.

It had been such an orderly existence until the time of that particular Dayspan.

As usual, she had been spending early Dayspan food-finding with other Stoopmothers in an area of the Great Gloom much favoured for its wild lushbobs.

A ground-shake was not unusual, and only rarely did one cause any damage, but this one had been different. Not only had it caused four old Rocktrees to fall, but a great crack had opened across the Way which leads to the Darkness.

Most chilling of all, as the last rumblings had left the Treelands of the Great Gloom, and echoed out across the flat, bright plains of the Glowurld, every Stoop had lifted a head in alarm, peering, jerkily, hen-like, in every direction, hardly daring to believe what their sensitive eyes were telling them – that the Light from the Glowurld was slowly, ever so slowly, fading.

The Dayspan had had many Lighthours left,

and yet the Light had begun to fade, and as the Stoopmothers had warily gathered their young ones and prepared to return to their hollows, there had come a fearsome and continuous howling from the Darkness as the loathsome Gork, too, had sensed the change.

Since that Dayspan there had been a steady decline in the amount of Light penetrating into the Great Gloom from the Glowurld.

Light was so important to the Stoop.

It ruled their lives.

It gave them a sense of place and distance; they could tell by the amount of Light how near or how far they were from their hollows; they knew each tree by the amount of Light it reflected; they knew how near they might be to the Darkness, and the pain in their eyes told them when they wandered too near to the Glowurld.

At the end of each Dayspan, when the Light died, Stoop would spend the Blacktime safe in their hollows, whilst above, the dreaded Gork roamed, enemies of all creatures of the Drabwurld, hunting and killing where they could, until the arrival of the Lightime drove them back into the Darkness, for their eyes could stand no Light at all.

But now, since the Dayspan of the great ground-shake, all things had changed.

Suddenly, Blid and the other Stoop found that even in the Lighthours they had to enlarge their eyes in an effort to take in what Light was left, and each span saw them having to wander further and further from the safety of their hollows, towards the Glowurld, in order to have enough Light to find food by.

Then, one day, Blid, with her friend Plin, had seen a strange sight. Looking up from their work on a foodbush, they had seen, well . . . nothing.

No trees, no rocks, nothing to interrupt their vision.

It took a while for them to realize that they were standing on the very edge of the Great Gloom, and looking out across the flat, empty plains of the Glowurld.

It was then that Blid realized just how much the Light had faded. Never before had a Stoop been able to look into the Glowurld during the Lighthours as she and Plin did on that day, and the emptiness they saw there reflected the emptiness and dread they felt inside.

Blid dragged her mind back to the present as Brog stirred in his sleep, and she shushed him reassuringly until he settled again. She remembered sleep from when she herself was a Stoopling, but now, as an adult, she no longer needed it.

She gazed at Brog.

Nor would he need it soon; his limbs were getting long, and when time for the change to adult came it would be swift and complete – from Stoopling to mature adult in the space of one Dayspan.

Her face clouded: Dayspan . . .

Would it mean the same, ever again?

There were parts of the Great Gloom that had become so dark that they had become unrecognizable, and the great concern voiced amongst the Stoop was that the lack of Light would cause the Gork to wander from their Darkness into Stoop territory.

But each Stoop took comfort from the knowledge that while there was any Light left at all, even just a glimmer, they were safe, for no Gork had ever been known to operate unless in blackness, or by the watery light of the double moons which hung like transparent bubbles in the sky.

Such was the nature of the Gork. They were creatures of blackness – black in soul, and black in deed.

Blid came alert suddenly as her keen ears detected a slithering at the entrance to her hollow, and with a soft click, her talons slid, gleaming, from the ends of her fingers.

Her crest arose, and she tensed every muscle,

placing herself defensively between the entrance and her young one.

Two eyes peered in, and a figure thrust its way forward under the roots.

Blid relaxed. It was Plin, her friend. No, more than a friend, closer than a sister. They had shared many happy moments when they were younger, and had comforted each other in times of tragedy.

Plin had borne a female young one, Lin, at the same Birthtime as Brog.

Lin had been Brog's constant playmate until the fateful time when she had wandered in her sleep from Plin's hollow, and had disappeared.

All evidence suggested that she had been taken by the Gork. It was not unknown for them to take female Stooplings and to enslave them, and Plin felt, somehow, that she *was* still alive.

Brog still thought of her often; they had been destined to be Breedmates when they both reached maturity, and he had made up his mind long ago that when he became a Stoopwarrior he would go into the Darkness and find her.

Plin, with Blid's help, had finally come to terms with her loss, and fought bravely, with each new span, to conceal from those around her the sadness she would always feel.

Today, however, the usual smile was missing from Plin's face and Blid could sense that there was something wrong, but she waited until Plin settled before asking what her news was.

Plin heaved a sigh. "An Elder Stoop has been taken," she said, gravely, "by the Gork."

This was bad news indeed, but Plin had more.

"He was taken . . ." She paused, aware of the significance of what she was about to say, "he was taken within the Great Gloom territory, and in the Lightime."

Blid drew breath sharply.

So, it had begun. The border areas of the Great Gloom had become dark enough for the Gorks to hunt in.

Now, no one would be safe.

Brog started and sat up, rubbing his eyes.

Blid clasped him to her.

"Your hollow and mine are not five hundred leaps from the border with the Darkness. In the Blacktime we hear them overhead, but if we are to hide from them in the Lightime too . . ."

Plin nodded Blid's last words away, and laid a paw on her friend's arm.

"There is to be a Council at the Flatplace. The Stoop are gathering even now. All things will be settled there. Come, we must away."

She turned and led them from the hollow,

Blid following close behind, with Brog crawling up into the weak, early Light behind his mother.

Brog, standing upright, was indeed tall for his age, reaching well above his mother's waist, with long, sinewy legs which promised strength in adulthood.

By tradition, Stooplings would stay with their mother until the very day of their swift change to adulthood, and, although there would always be a strong bond between mother and Stoop, never again afterwards would he share her hollow or rely upon her for food.

The three made their way swiftly through the trees, glancing eternally left to right, wary and alert, and the knee-high mist closed behind them as they cut a furrow through it.

Abruptly, the trees ended, and they entered a huge circular clearing of flatland.

This was the Flatplace; carved out of the Treelands countless Moonruns ago, and used ever since for Stoop Councils at time of great crisis.

From edge to edge it was thronged with Stoop of all ages, faces turned towards the centre where a series of large, flat rocks were arranged at different levels.

At ground level there were ten, and each had standing upon it a Stoopwarrior in full battlewood – breastplate, shoulder, arm, and shin pads all giving off the dull, silken gleam of the rockwood from which they were fashioned. From their belts hung the deadly, short, sharp stabbing-sword of dense Magnatree – the Ka'thuk.

The second level of flat rocks numbered six, and these too were occupied by warriors, whose adornments showed that they were Division Leaders.

Three more rocks were on a level above them. These held the Marshals, even more finely adorned.

Higher again, stood the three Stoopwarriors Supreme, Stoop of impeccable fighting quality and proven valour, revered by all.

The topmost rock was almost as high as the surrounding treetops, and its occupant gazed nobly out over the heads of the gathered tribe.

He was a magnificent creature, finely proportioned, long-legged and elegant, with wide, muscular shoulders and a proud head from which hung a mane of blond hair.

His battlewood was of the finest blond Magna, and the Ka'thuk which hung from his belt was so highly polished that it gleamed like the surface of the nearby lake, catching the pitiful Light which was struggling through the trees.

This was the Stooplord. This was Klan the Golden!

Blid and Plin, with Brog between them, pushed their way through to the front of the murmuring crowd to an area where a number of other Stoopmothers stood with their young.

These were the mothers who, with Blid and Plin, had all borne their young at the same Birthtime.

On the far side of the Flatplace stood the more recent Birthgroup, younger by five seasons and, consequently, much smaller than Brog and his contemporaries.

Blid was always so proud whenever Brog was in a crowd. He stood out amongst the others of his age, being taller than they, and his bearing seemed to command attention.

Plin was almost as proud of him herself, remembering the time when he and her own lost Stoopling, Lin, had been inseparable.

Brog went straight to the side of another Stoopling, almost as well-proportioned as himself, a smile of welcome on his broad, bright face.

"Pik!" Brog greeted his friend. "I hoped you'd be here."

"Who isn't here?" returned Pik, looking around him. "This must be the biggest Council ever called!"

Pik it was who had loved Lin as a sister, and had felt her loss almost as much as Brog himself.

The three had shared adventures together, laughed and tumbled through the Great Gloom, swam in the lake with the kind of joyous abandonment that only true friends know.

Pik it was who had vowed to accompany Brog in his search for Lin as soon as their growing time was through, and it was Pik whose trust and friendship Brog cherished more than that of any other.

The air quivered as a blast from the huge meeting horn thundered over their heads, and all eyes turned to the Stooplord standing proudly on the topmost flatrock.

Brog gazed in admiration. "When my Growtime comes, I want to be just like him," he whispered.

Pik snorted good-humouredly. "Brog, you dreamer. There can only ever be one Klan! One Stooplord!"

Brog nodded. "A dream will be enough – for now." He smiled.

For a long time, Klan surveyed the sea of upturned faces, and when he eventually spoke, his voice was rich and powerful.

"Stoop!" he began. "We gather here to decide what we must do!"

He turned slowly as he spoke, throwing his voice to the far edges of the circle.

"The Light from the Glowurld is dying. As

the Light dies, so the Darkness spreads." A pause. "With the Darkness come the Gork!"

A murmur of dread rippled over the crowd, fading as Klan continued.

"Let me hear your voices. What do the Stoop people say must be done?"

Several Stoop began to push their way forward, all making for a low platform at the base of the flatrocks.

There they gathered, and, after a signal from Klan, the first faced the crowd and began to speak. He was a battle-scarred veteran, and his tone was bitter.

"I am Goth, from the Far-Region."

The murmurs ceased. Goth was well known.

"In two Dayspans, we have lost four people to the Gork from the Darkness. So weak is the Light, that only the treeless areas are safe to walk in. We of the Far-Region say it is time to leave our hollows and move to the fringe of the Glowurld!"

Goth's supporters made their agreement known, shouting and banging swords on breastplates.

A second Stoop stepped up.

"I am Dork!" he began. "What are we? Scutterlings, afraid of our own shadows? Rock-beetles, hiding from an upturned stone? We are Stoop! We do not desert our homes when danger threatens! All Stoop from the Mid-Region vote to stay and fight!"

A great roar followed his speech.

Pik turned to Brog. "He is right!"

Brog mused. "Maybe," he said.

"Maybe?!" spat Pik, amazed at Brog's doubt. "You heard him – we are Stoop!"

"We are Stoop," said Brog, quietly, "only while we have Light."

The next speaker was an Elder, and he spoke more quietly, obviously trying to bring calm to the meeting, for feelings were beginning to run high.

"One thing only do we know," he began, "nothing is for always. Just as the Light is dying, I believe one day it will return. We must wait and watch until that day."

There were snorts of exasperation from the other speakers, but the old Stoop continued.

"If we move to the fringe of the Glowurld, where do we move if the Light becomes even less? Into the Glowurld itself?"

"Aye! If we have to!" Goth roared in frustration.

The old Stoop turned to him, looked him straight in the eye.

"And then. . . ?" he said, simply.

There was silence as realization fell upon the listeners.

The truth was that if the Light continued to fade, there would, eventually, be nowhere to go.

Murmurs of consternation ran through the crowd, growing to a buzz of anxiety.

A lone voice cut through the uncertainty, a clear, determined voice.

It belonged to Brog.

"I wish to speak!"

He was directing his statement to Klan the Golden, the Stooplord himself.

Pik took his arm, alarmed.

"Brog, you can't!" he hissed.

All around, heads were turning, Stoop craning to see who it was that had spoken from the floor and not from the platform.

Blid stepped up to Brog, concern showing clearly on her face.

"Brog!" She tried to speak low. "This is Council! You are but a Stoopling!"

But Brog was committed. He lifted his head again and spoke, no sign of fear in his voice.

"If Klan will allow me . . ." he said.

Klan looked down sternly, and for a moment Brog *was* afraid, then suddenly, Klan smiled and indicated the speaking platform. Triumphantly, Brog stepped forward. The crowd muttered, puzzled: a Stoopling addressing Council? Unheard of!

Once on the platform, Brog took a deep

breath, and turned to face the whole Stoop nation.

They settled to listen.

From close behind him, Dork snorted impatiently. Whatever Brog had to say, it would have to be good.

"Who knows what is the Light?" Brog asked them. "Who knows what makes the Light?" And then, answering his own question, "No one!"

His voice was strong, and echoed back to him from the dense trees at the far edges of the circle.

"And so," he continued, "we stand helpless as the Light dies. We must learn of its sickness if we are to cure it."

Dork's voice roared over Brog's head, and there was no mistaking his contempt.

"The Light?" he cried. "The Light *is* – and always has been! We will not defeat the Gork by questioning the Light!"

But Brog matched his fervour, word for word.

"Do we not hunt better the Slithercat because we know the ways of the Slithercat? Do we not, from Dayspan to Dayspan, evade the Gork because we know the ways of the Gork?"

Heads were beginning to nod in agreement.

"So," continued Brog, "we must know the Light. Only then can we tell what is to be done."

"You talk not sense, Stoopling, the Light is not for questioning," retorted Dork. "No one knows of the Light!"

The Elder Stoop who had spoken earlier broke in.

"There is one who knows," he said, gently, "and only one – we must approach the Drab-keeper."

Dork threw back his head and gave a short, sharp laugh of derision.

"Hah! The Drabkeeper?" he hooted. "No one in living memory has seen the Drabkeeper! Many even question his existence!" He turned, in exasperation, to Klan. "My Lord . . ."

"He does exist!" cried Brog. "I know it! And the Elder speaks true, he can help us!"

"He can advise us," corrected the Elder. "Our destinies are of our own making."

Dork threw up his paws in frustration. Brog persisted.

"Look what will happen, else," he argued. "In all of the Drabwurld there is but one creature who can survive without the Light. The Gork! If the Light is lost, the Gork will have total rule!"

Dissent broke out.

Goth and Dork began to argue their original points, but their voices were lost as, suddenly, everyone began to make themselves heard, and the noise-level gradually rose.

Brog glanced down at Pik who gave him a "well done" fist of support.

As far as could be seen, Stoop were arguing, gesticulating, calling for action of one kind or another.

The disorder continued only until Klan raised his arms in appeal, and the crowd slowly muttered into a silence.

Klan spoke.

"I have listened," he said, and paused for effect. "The Stoopling Brog speaks well."

Brog's face showed the amazement he felt – that the Stooplord should know his name!

"We must learn of the sickness of the Light. We must find, and approach, the Drabkeeper. But now, we must return to our hollows and prepare to defend ourselves. Every Stoop must carry arms against the enemy. Plans must be made . . ."

He stopped abruptly, and all eyes turned to him.

The Stooplord had become suddenly alert.

Brog watched him as he crouched atop his flatrock, his crest risen, hand upon his sword, eyes darting left and right, head moving jerkily from side to side, nostrils sniffing the breeze. Immediately, the Stoopwarriors on the lower flatrocks took up similar positions, peering into the Treelands from their vantage points.

Amongst the crowd there spread an uneasiness at this display of warning signs, but it was an uneasiness mixed with genuine puzzlement. They knew that they had only one predator, but they also knew that, with Light in the sky, however feeble, they were safe, for it was a known fact that Gork simply could not stand any trace of Dayspan Light.

Nevertheless, instincts are strong, and despite themselves, all around could be heard the soft click of female claws being exposed. Crests were rising on heads, and anxiety spread. Something was wrong.

There was a disturbance to the right on the fringe of the trees, as to Blid's nostrils came the faint, but unmistakable smell of . . . Gork!

The attack was sudden, swift, and incredibly savage.

Twenty-five Gork roared in from the right, screaming and slashing as they came.

Those Stoop nearest to the point of attack stood no chance.

Forty others attacked from the left flank of the gathering with equal ferocity, whilst from the back came the blood-chilling roars of a third group as it tore its way into the stunned and amazed crowd.

Many Stoop, for vital seconds, were rooted to the spot, unable to believe what they were seeing. Then the crowd scattered in every direction, Stoopmothers gathering their young as they fled. Male Stoop gathered in clusters, protecting the female and young, and hurling themselves, many unarmed, at the invaders.

Brog had never actually seen a Gork before, though he knew well what they should look like, from countless stories and pictures drawn by his mother, but somehow, these Gork seemed different. There was something about them which did not tally with the description he had in his mind; something more than just the livid white stripe across the forehead of each – a feature which had never figured in any description that he had ever heard.

They were bigger than he had expected them to be, and faster. Deceptively fast, in fact, for such bulky creatures.

Brog was swept along with the mass of bodies, each trying desperately to keep out of reach of the savage enemy.

In the crush, he lost sight of Blid, and of Plin and Pik, and he fought to catch sight of them in the crowd.

He was able to catch only glimpses of what was happening as he was carried along.

In the few minutes since the attack had begun, the Stoop had suffered heavy losses, and bodies seemed to be strewn everywhere.

Klan and his warriors could be seen fighting valiantly in a number of places, supported by bands of plain Stoop, swords flashing, making full use of their superior speed of foot, and more than one Gork fell screaming.

Brog felt so utterly helpless, and wished with all his heart that he could be fighting like them instead of merely struggling to keep upright in the surge of fleeing bodies.

One Gork stood out amongst the rest.

He was half as big again as any of the others, and seemed to be directing operations from a point in the centre of the Flatplace, but the single feature which really separated him from his murderous counterparts was his eyes, and Brog's blood ran cold as he saw them.

The eyes of this giant Gork were pure evil, piercing, and a bright, glowing red!

As the Stoop reached the trees, the crowd thinned, and Brog found he had time to stand and look around for familiar faces.

Klan and his band were fighting a brave, but losing battle, and were being driven nearer and nearer to the trees at the far side of the clearing. It was obvious that, in a matter of minutes, they too would be forced to break off and retreat, though the time they had bought by their brave actions had been invaluable.

Brog scanned the passing faces, searching for

some hope that Blid and the others had escaped the dreadful slaughter, but nowhere could he see those he had lost.

"Brog! Brog!" A shout to his right.

It was Pik, and he was beckoning furiously from the fringe of the trees.

In the centre of the Flatplace, Redeye turned his head as he heard the voice, and saw the tall, young Stoopling run across, making for the fringe.

His Gork had done well, many Stoop lay dead, the Stoopwarriors were being driven to retreat.

A little killing of his own would be quite pleasant.

Turning, he lumbered in pursuit of the Stoopling, fangs bared in a snarl.

From the corner of his eye, Brog saw Redeye moving to the attack, and he put in a burst of speed. Redeye gave a roar, fearing that his victim was about to escape him, and changed the angle of his charge in an effort to cut him off.

"Faster, Brog, faster!" urged Pik.

Brog's long legs were covering the ground at a tremendous pace, and it was touch and go whether he reached the trees before, or at the same time as Redeye.

A figure hurtled past Brog from out of the

bushes, too fast for him to see who it was, but he heard the roar of surprise from Redeye, and the thud of bodies behind him before he was grabbed by Pik, and dragged, still running, into the thickness of the Treelands.

Redeye tore viciously at the Stoopmother who had prevented him from catching the speeding young one and, knowing that she had made Brog's escape possible, Blid died.

CHAPTER 2

6rog ran blindly through the Treelands, oblivious to everything but the need to get as far away as possible from the carnage he had just witnessed.

The branches lashed his face as he ran, but he felt no pain; the breath was wrenched from his lungs in great sobs as he weaved and ducked and tore his way through the greenery, until at last, unable to move another step and utterly exhausted, he fell to the floor of the forest, panting and gasping like a stranded Mogfish.

How long he lay there it was impossible to say, but long after his heaving chest had subsided and his breathing had returned to normal, the vivid pictures of the slaughter flashed across his mind and sent his heart pounding in his ears, and he hugged the ground for comfort. The feel of the soil beneath his fingers reassured him that he was, in fact, alive.

Blid. Where was Blid? And Pik. Pik had been right behind him, where was he now?

He listened.

Silence, deep and oppressive.

He opened his eyes.

The weak shadows were long, he had run for most of the span, and there was not much of it left. The Blackhours were not far away. It was then that the guilt began to disturb him. He had given way to blind panic, reason had deserted him, and the feeling was not a good one.

Now that he was relatively calm and able to think more clearly, he began to wish with all his heart that he could relive the last few hours; even if it meant giving his life, it would be preferable to the miserable contempt he felt for himself right now.

A rustle in the undergrowth to his left startled him, and he sat up, holding his breath.

There it was again, nearer this time.

He sprang to one knee, alert, determined this time, if necessary, to sell his life dearly, to make up in some way, if need be, for his performance earlier on.

He grabbed a fallen branch as a weapon, and waited, watching in the direction from which the sound had come, his apprehension mingling with anger and loathing for the beasts who had attacked his people in so cowardly a fashion.

A bush twitched; Brog gripped his branch tighter.

The bush parted, and he found himself staring into the bloodstained face of the one person he least expected to see – Klan the Golden, Lord of the Stoop.

"Klan!" whispered Brog, inclining his head in the traditional show of respect.

Klan had his wounds, but he bore them well, and the bright green bloodstains on his breastplate bore witness to the Gork he had slain.

For a moment he stood in silence, and Brog lowered his own eyes, wondering if his Stooplord knew that he had run from the battlefield, but Klan's countenance was kindly, and gave no hint of reproach.

Suddenly, "Come," said Klan, and turned away into the trees, breaking almost at once into a hunter's lope.

Brog followed, loping as Klan did in that steady, rhythmical, measured pace used by Stoop since time began, a pace which covered ground swiftly and economically, and was designed to keep the quarry in sight, but not to tire the hunter.

Stooplings learned it from very young, and Brog's fine, long legs were particularly well adapted to it.

He kept his eyes on the broad back and shoulders of Klan, and concentrated on the regular push, push, push of his own stride, digging his three-toed feet into the soil for grip.

They ran until the Blackhours made it impossible to see, then they rested, Klan ever watchful, with his eyes as large as he could make them, and Brog, still just too young to go without some sleep, curled in the shelter of an overhang in the rock face. And all the time, not a word was spoken.

Brog's last thought, before sleep overtook him, was of his mother, Blid. She would be searching for him.

He awoke before the Lighthours came.

Klan was exactly as he had last seen him, crouched, motionless, his bodycells regenerating, only the quick darting of his eyes, and the twitch of an ear telling that he was alert.

As the weak rays of the Lighthours began a new span, they ate a hurried meal of lushbobs and culweed, and it was then that Brog broke the long silence.

"Lord Klan," began Brog, nervously, "why do we travel, and where?"

Klan finished the berries he had before replying.

"To a place known to few," he said, simply. "From here we climb, it will be hard . . . come." And with that, he sprang to his feet, leaving Brog no alternative but to follow.

Hard it was.

All that span they climbed and ran, ran and climbed, Klan setting the pace, and Brog using all his young strength and agility to keep up.

Thoughts raced through his head.

Why was Klan taking him so far from his homeland?

What had happened to the people he knew and loved?

Had they escaped as he had done?

The Gork!

His eyes blazed as he thought of them! How had they, the creatures of Darkness, been able to attack in the Lighthours?

And Redeye!

However he tried, Brog could not drive the thought of the evil giant from his mind, and even though the sweat was on his brow, he felt chilled to the bone.

So bound up was he in his thoughts as he

ran, he failed to notice that the Lightime had begun to slip away again.

The spans were so short now.

They began to enlarge their eyes, and ran on for a short while longer before Klan called a halt.

Although it was now too dark to see, Brog knew from his aching muscles that they were on very high ground.

Brog woke from his shallow sleep fitfully and often, his mind a turmoil of images. Once, he awoke with a start to find Klan sitting beside him with a smile on his lips and a faraway look in his eyes.

"What is it?" Brog muttered sleepily.

"Nothing, Brog, nothing," Klan murmured. "Sleep your sleep, capture your strength. You will be in need of it."

And Brog slept.

The Lightime showed just how high they had climbed; it seemed to Brog that they were on the very roof of the world.

The whole of the Drabwurld lay at their feet, the Light barely penetrating the thick Treelands of the Great Gloom below, and beyond, black and foreboding, Brog could see the dreaded Darkness, with trees and rocks so densely packed that no Light whatever was able to creep into that evil zone.

Looking down on the opposite side of the

mountain on which they stood, the panorama could not have been more of a contrast: stretched as far as the eye could see, the sparse, level plains of the Glowurld lay like a blanket.

With not a tree or a rock to interrupt its passage, the pale, sickly Light spread, butter-like, from the horizon to the fringes of the Drabwurld at their feet.

The only feature of any prominence was the distant outline of a mountain range, rising like giant fingers pointing to the sky, and beyond that, a glow still too bright for Brog to look at — the very Source of all Light.

The air was sweet and clean, and nearby ran a crystal-clear stream.

Klan was washing his wounds as Brog approached him.

"Lord Klan," he said, "where is this?"

Klan sat on a rock, and Brog did likewise.

"This," began the Stooplord, "is the Uplands, the highest point of the Drabwurld. Here the Light will last longer. Here you are safe."

Brog made to speak, but Klan held up a hand. His voice softened.

"Your mother, Blid. . . ." He hesitated. "She is no more."

Brog drew breath sharply.

Klan continued. "Her life was taken in the attack. She died to save you."

Brog felt a sadness like a heavy stone on his chest, and struggled to show no emotion before his Stooplord.

Now he knew who it was that had rushed by him when Redeye was on his tail. His hate for the monster grew deeper, and his resolve for revenge so acute he could almost taste it.

He realized that Klan was talking to him, and focused his attention.

"I know of your sadness, Brog. I share your sadness, for Blid was my Breedmate of many Moonruns."

Brog's eyes widened in surprise.

Stoopmothers could have only one Breedmate, that was Stoop law. They could also only bear one Stoopling.

He, Brog, was Blid's Stoopling. His mind raced ahead of him . . . if Klan was the Breedmate of Blid, then he . . .

Klan answered his unspoken question.

"I am your father," he said.

Brog was stunned. To lose a mother and to find a father in so short a space of time was almost more than he could take in. Klan waited, allowing time for Brog to digest the news, only continuing when the acknowledgement on Brog's face told him that he fully understood.

"We have work to do, you and I," said Klan. "Never before have our people faced such a danger. Only the return of the Light from the Glowurld will drive the Gork back to the Darkness. Until that time, we must rally and fight them for every inch of the Great Gloom."

Brog eyed his father determinedly. "I am ready," he said, grimly.

Klan laid a hand on his shoulder. "How deep is your belief in the Drabkeeper?" he asked.

Brog didn't even hesitate in his reply.

"I see him in the winds that cool, in the trees which shelter us. He is the order of things, the beat and rhythm of our lives. To me, he is as real as . . . as you."

Klan nodded, and a smile curled the corners of his mouth.

"Your belief tells me that there is yet hope." He stood. "I will return to the people. Your work is here, my son."

Brog began to protest, but Klan continued. "Your task is more important than mine." He indicated their surroundings. "Somewhere here is the home of that one creature who may be able to tell us of a way to return the Light. The Drabkeeper. You must find him. Find him and plead for his help. If you will do this, then for all Stoop there is still hope, and our fight can take on a meaning." He looked Brog straight in the eyes. "Will you do it?"

Brog rose to his feet and, not for the first time,

Klan admired his height, and the sturdy build of his frame.

"If I have to search each rock, valley and mountain peak, I will find the Drabkeeper, and I will bring to you his word."

Klan smiled grimly, and nodded in satisfaction.

"And now I must go," he said, "there are Gork to slay, battles to be won." He squeezed Brog's arm . . . "Blid to avenge."

He girded his sword tighter, and prepared to move off.

Brog accompanied him to the start of the descent. Klan clasped Brog's shoulders in his huge paws, and looked proudly into the face that was suddenly so like his own.

"It may be a lonely time for you, Brog," he said. "Those with responsibilities like yours and mine are often lonely. It is the price we must pay as leaders of the people."

He turned to go, hesitated, and looked back. "We depend on you, Brog. I know the son of Klan will not desert us."

And without another word, he began the long descent.

Brog watched him until he was but a speck in the distance, then turned and strode purposefully up the hill.

CHAPTER 3

The silence lay like a heavy cloak. Pik crouched motionless at the base of the Rocktree which stood by the Way which leads to the Darkness.

There, on the other side of the Way, waiting just as intently as he, Pik could make out his six companions, death-quiet but alert, tensed for the action they knew must come their way very soon now.

For three hours, Pik, with Dork-el, son of Dork and the other five who made up the raiding party, had waited, watched as the last of the Gork had trundled from the Darkness on their way into the Great Gloom to search out Stoop to murder.

All the Gork had been of the NewBreed, the livid white stripe to be seen clearly across the loathsome face, tiny eyes glinting in the weak Light for which they had been especially bred.

Snaked across the Way, between Pik and Dork-el, lay the twist of stranglevine they had fashioned for the job in hand; it blended well with the ground, and in the dimness was all but invisible. Sooner or later the Gork would begin to return to rest in the Darkness, and their places would be taken by the OldBreed, the night hunters.

Now, towards the end of the Dayspan, while the Light was still in their favour but at its most dim, Pik and his band intended to strike.

Since the Gork attack at the Flatplace three spans ago, much had happened.

In the absence of the Stooplord Klan, Dork had gathered what remained of the Stoop, and they had taken refuge in the rockholes of the huge Sheerstone which rose high above the Treelands close by the edge of the Glowurld.

The entrances to the rockholes were few and easy to defend, and here the Stoopmothers and Stooplings could remain in safety, venturing out only to collect food, whilst the young Stoop and warriors, in small fighting groups, went out to raid the enemy with what weapons they could find.

For Pik, and the other newly matured Stoop, this was to be their first taste of action, and each desperately wanted their trap to succeed; each wanted revenge for their loved ones killed so brutally at the Flatplace, and each was prepared to sacrifice his life, if necessary, in the fight to be a free people once again.

As he waited, Pik's thoughts went to Brog.

Was he alive or dead?

No one had seen him since his close escape from Redeye, and Pik's heart burned with sadness at the thought that he might never see his friend again.

Even more puzzling had been Klan's disappearance.

The battle had ended with surprising suddenness, and the Gork had melted into the trees on the command of Redeye, but even before the sound of their great bodies crashing through the foliage had died away, Klan had sped into the Treelands.

Since then, no one had seen him, and there were those who questioned his going, saying he had deserted his people when they needed him most.

In his heart, Pik knew this could not be true.

Klan was the greatest Warrior-Lord the Stoop had ever had, and whatever his reasons for leaving the battlefield, Pik knew they would be honourable ones.

Until Klan's return, Pik saw his duty was to avenge those who had died at the Battle of the Flatplace – and to kill as many Gork as he could find.

If only he had Brog to fight by his side.

The grip on his dagger tightened as he tried to push the thought from his mind that Brog might no longer be alive, that he might have been killed as Blid was, and on the very eve of his maturity.

There came a crunch some distance along the Way, and Pik's ears swivelled in that direction, cupping to catch the sound. Crunch, again.

He clicked his tongue to catch the attention of the others, and Dork-el signalled that they too had heard it.

With his end of the stranglevine between his teeth, Pik swiftly climbed the rocktree.

Dork-el, likewise, climbed the tree opposite, and there they crouched, eyes enlarged, ears twitching, waiting, the stranglevine lying loosely on the ground between them.

The smell reached them first, as it always did, and their crests rose as the hated stench reached their nostrils, then, faintly at first, they caught the first glimpses of the Gork as he approached along the winding Way to where they waited.

He was big, even for a NewBreed, maybe as high as four Stoop, and Pik sucked breath through his teeth as he saw the jutting, yellow fangs, dripping with saliva.

Pik looked to Dork-el, and they shared a nod of satisfaction; the head would be almost on a level with them as it passed.

Slowly, the unsuspecting Gork lumbered along, drawing ever nearer, the powerful tail scraping the ground as he strode, looking lazily from side to side as he came.

Nearer . . . nearer . . . nearer . . . Pik and Dork-el tensed, waiting the moment to strike.

No more than two leaps from the trees they were hiding in, the Gork suddenly stopped, became alert, tiny, evil eyes darting furiously about, and a low growl rose from his huge chest. He had sensed danger and swung his head from side to side, scanning the area in detail.

The two young Stoop held their breath. The foliage in the trees was sparse and offered little cover and it was only a matter of time before they were spotted.

Below them, a Stoop broke from the bush and scampered away in a brave attempt to draw the Gork forward.

The beast took a step, roared, but moved no further; instead, his spiked tail swept the bush on either side of the Way, searching for his enemy, too intelligent to be lured into any trap, hungry for the blood of whoever he sensed was threatening him.

The tail thudded against Dork-el's tree, vibrating the upper branches alarmingly, and, with a cry, Dork-el fell virtually at the feet of the monster.

Even before Dork-el hit the ground, Pik's dagger was out and hurtling towards the Gork. It struck, and dug deep into the neck; not a life-threatening wound, but enough to divert the creature's attention and enable Dork-el to regain his feet.

Swiftly, Pik leapt from his perch, the strangle-vine in his hand, his supple legs giving him the spring he needed to land, with a slap of the feet, momentarily on the Gork's slimy back, before continuing, with a second spring, to the ground on his far side. The Gork whirled and Dork-el, seizing his chance, whipped the stranglevine over the massive head, making a loop around its neck.

The Gork spun rapidly, using its tail again to clear the ground around it. Bushes and young trees were scattered like feathers, and Pik and Dork-el leapt in the air to allow the tail to pass beneath their feet. Another Stoop, misjudging the ferocity of the enemy's retaliation, was caught and sent hurtling high in the air, to land with a bone-crunching thud many strides away.

For a moment, the Gork hesitated, uncertain which of its two main tormentors to attack first, its evil eyes flickering from one to the other, lips curled back in a snarl, saliva hanging thread-like from the gaping jaws, then, with a speed which made a mockery of its size, it lunged savagely at the nearest – Pik.

The young Stoop came within a sword's thickness of death; so close did that terrible mouth come that he felt the hot stench of its breath dry the moisture from his eyeballs.

Only just in time, he threw himself aside, realizing as he straightened up the advantage that the Gork's action had given him.

At his feet lay the coils of slack stranglevine, and in the time it took for the Gork to recover its balance, Pik had gathered it and wrapped it speedily around the trunk of the nearest tree. Furious at having missed its target, the creature turned, the muscles in its hind legs bulging as it thrust its whole weight this time in the direction of Dork-el.

The stranglevine came taut, snapping back the Gork's head, and the ground shook as the beast came crashing down.

Dork-el expertly whipped another loop over the Gork's head as it struggled to regain its feet, and the other Stoop made fast the end to the same tree.

The realization that it was tethered sent the Gork into a frenzy of blind panic, and the Treelands rang with the echo of the roars as it thrashed and twisted, lashing out with its tail in all directions.

The Stoop knew that the kill must be made in as short a time as possible now; other Gork would have heard the commotion, and would soon be on the scene.

Keeping just out of range, circling the beast, they waited for the opportunity to launch their thick-shafted throwstiks from the sling that always hung from their forearm.

The stranglevine had tightened around the beast's neck, and it was breathing with difficulty as Pik sent in the first throwstik, a true shot to the chest, delivered with venom, and helped on the way by the thought of the slaughter at the Flatplace.

A half dozen more throws from Pik's companions finished the job, and the loathsome creature shuddered and subsided, the last hissing breath rasping coarsely in its throat.

In the silence that followed, the group gazed on their enemy, and led by Pik, they began to stamp their left feet in unison, in the Stoop victory salute.

The Stoop hit by the Gork's tail had been badly hurt, and arrangements were made to carry him back to the rockholes of the Sheerstone; meanwhile, the throwstiks had been recovered from the Gork's body, and the stranglevine cut from its neck and coiled ready to be put to further good use.

With a final glance at their enemy, the party turned and began to pad away, the Darkness at their backs, their eyes set upon that lighter part of the sky where lay the rockholes of the Sheerstone and the remainder of the Stoop nation.

Not a word was said, but each shared the satisfaction of knowing that they had rid the Great Gloom of one more evil predator.

With a roar that shook the trees, the Gork they thought dead rose and launched itself in fury at the departing band, eyes blazing, mouth wide, the razor-sharp claws flailing the air.

Caught completely unawares, and stunned with surprise, the Stoop were slow to react, and not one managed to draw his Ka'thuk before the beast was upon them.

They were at his mercy.

From the Treelands flew a throwstik, wickedly pointed, magnificently fashioned from blond Magnawood, a weighted gold collar at the base of the point.

It whistled over their heads and buried itself to the collar in the forehead of the Gork.

Its roar was cut so cleanly that the sound still hung in the air as the body crashed to the ground, lifeless.

They turned, knowing as they did that there could only be one person to thank for the marksmanship that had just saved them from death.

The throwstik was instantly recognizable.

Klan the Golden, the Stooplord, had returned!

CHAPTER 4

With the first, faint Light of the new Day-span, Brog awoke and knew that the sleep he had just had would be the last he would ever experience.

During the Blackhours, the skin on his arms, legs, and back had begun to split, and the new, metallic bluey-green shine of his adult skin beneath was already showing through.

Soon he would shed the old skin, and with it, the need for sleep.

All that span he stayed in his hollow.

He felt weak and lethargic, in a kind of half-state, his mind beset with confused images of all that had happened over the past few spans.

From time to time he fancied he saw shapes, images, at the opening of his hollow; faces, some of which he recognized – Lin, Pik, Blid. Others were strangers, weird, plant-like, looking in on him. But each time he peered closer, they disappeared into a haze. He heard laughter, too, thin, high-pitched, piping laughter, like the sound of water running over rocks; and all the time the splits in his old skin got wider and wider, and it began to fall away.

It was not until the middle of the following Blacktime that he began to feel more clearheaded.

Gradually the 'muzziness' withdrew from him, and a new feeling of purpose seemed to establish itself deep within.

He squatted on his haunches, staring unblinkingly into the dark, the cool, still air wafting from the opening.

He drank in the silence, his ears twitching every now and then, as their new, sharp focus caught the scuffle of some nocturnal creature in the fields.

The Blacktime, to the Stoop, is a time of regeneration, a time to replenish the energies burned away during the Dayspan, a time of calm and serenity, and Brog's first taste of it was like a drink from an icy mountain stream.

As the meagre rays of Light chased away

the Blacktime, Brog stepped from his hollow.

If there had been anyone to witness the Stoopling who had entered it only one Dayspan before, they would not have recognized the tall, young Stoop who now emerged, as the same person.

The early Light, dim though it was, gleamed on the skin stretched tightly over his muscular chest and arms.

Broad shoulders rippled with strength, and he held his proud head high, a mane of blond hair cascading to his shoulders.

He flung wide his arms, flexing and stretching his re-formed body, and finally, eyes gleaming with intent, he threw back his head and gave a mighty roar at the sky.

He was, every inch, a Royal Stoop.

It was later that span, that Brog chose a rock, within sight of his hollow, and sat looking out over the Glowurld, turning over, again and again, the problem set for him by his father.

He had searched the land around for many, many strides, and had seen no evidence of habitation of any kind, no hollows, caves, or structures wherein might live anyone, let alone the Drabkeeper. Yet, despite this, his belief in the existence of the Drabkeeper was, if anything, even stronger. The Uplands had such an ordered beauty, there was nothing random or haphazard about it, and he felt, distinctly, the presence of the being responsible for that.

As he pondered, a movement caught his eye on the edges of his vision, and he turned quickly, but there was nothing. Instinct now confirmed the feeling he had had ever since he had come to the mountain – that he was not the only living creature in these parts.

He scanned the area around, and turned again, uneasily, to his reflections.

Another movement! This time to the left.

His keen eyes narrowed suspiciously as he took in every inch of the ground.

Again, nothing.

Nothing but the tall, red flowers which grew everywhere.

He looked back towards his hollow, and found, with alarm, that he could no longer see it, yet he had not shifted position.

His hollow was hidden from sight by scores of the red flowers.

He shook his head to clear his thoughts.

Something was wrong, he felt it, but knew not what it was. He rose, and slowly, nonchalantly, he strode back towards his hollow, purposely measuring his pace in a leisurely manner, to all appearances on a casual stroll.

Suddenly, after a half dozen strides, he whirled to face the other way.

For one micro-second, he could not believe his eyes – a host of small creatures were following him! He blinked and, just as suddenly, they were not there, just the knee-high red flowers, nodding and swaying.

Had he seen what, for a brief instant, he thought he had seen? Or was the dim Light and his imagination playing tricks with his eyes? As he stood wondering, again came the over-powering feeling that there was someone – some thing – behind him.

He whirled again, and again the same split-second vision of creatures melted into as many red flowers. But wait! There! To the left! Yes! A movement! Brog's head bobbed with eagerness to see what it was, he ran to the spot by a boulder.

And gasped in amazement at what he saw.

Whether it was plant or animal he could not tell, but it was most definitely a mixture of the two: a slender green body, with sloping shoulders, leading to two leaf-thin arms which waved in panic as it looked up at Brog with two enormous eyes set in a head as red and as round as the flowers which swayed around it. Two long, pointed ears stood up starkly, and the creature was stamping its many-toed feet in exasperation on an outcrop of rock from the boulder which just showed beneath the grass.

It was no taller than Brog's knee, and it cowered in fright as Brog bent to peer more closely at it.

Never had Brog seen anything like it and, far from wishing it harm, his heart went out to the little creature who obviously thought its days were numbered.

Wrapping its thin arms over its head, it began to shake.

Brog spoke to it in a voice that was as gentle and reassuring as he could make it. "Now, little creature, now, now, now," in the very way that Blid used to soothe away his own fears. "Do not fear, come, see, I mean you no harm."

The plant-animal only cowered further, blinking up at Brog beneath its leafy arms, the ends of which separated into what could only be three fingers, though they resembled leaves.

Brog shushed, and held out his own paw, palm upwards, in a gesture of friendliness.

"You are a strange being," chuckled Brog, half to himself, "so like a growing plant, yet so like an animal." He shook his head in wonder. "A . . . Planimal!"

Brog could not restrain a laugh, and the creature looked up in amazement as he heard the sound. The surprise on the Planimal's face could not be mistaken for fear, or anguish, or any other of the more likely emotions considering the plight it was in.

It stopped quaking, its arms around its head went limp, and it looked up at Brog with a blank expression, head cocked on one side, as though it could hardly believe what it had heard.

Brog was bemused, and the Planimal's new attitude caused Brog to chuckle again.

The Planimal dropped all semblance of defence and began to take an immediate interest.

"What is it, little fellow?" ventured Brog, and immediately regretted it, for the Planimal once more shrank from the sound of his voice.

Puzzled, Brog laughed again – this time on purpose.

The reaction was immediate, the Planimal once more became curious.

Brog was intrigued. A creature which was an obvious combination of plant and animal life was surely as strange as one could wish to find, but one which seemed to respond to laughter too, almost defied belief.

But stranger things were about to happen.

The Planimal looked intently into Brog's face, and, from somewhere inside its head, came the sound of thin, high-pitched laughter, or at least, what sounded to Brog like laughter, and at the same moment, Brog sensed that the little creature was talking to him; not only that, but Brog knew what it was saying. The words formed, clearly and precisely, in his head: "Who are you?"

It was then that Brog noticed the surrounding flowers.

They were changing, slowly, almost imperceptibly, but nevertheless, changing. All around him, leaves were becoming arms, stems were turning to bodies, eyes were opening in heads which, only moments before, had been a gathering of petals.

The flowers were becoming animals!

The air filled with the sound of their voices, laughter, piping and brittle, not unpleasant, rather like the chuckle of a thousand streams, and all of it, to Brog's amazement, meaningful to him. Without speaking a word, they were asking him a million questions: Where was he from? Did he have a name? What did he want? Did he mean them harm?

He was surrounded by them.

Smiling, Brog stood, and at once those nearest transformed in a twinkling back to their plant forms, only to emerge again, like frightened kittens, when they realized he meant them no harm.

Brog now had a problem.

How to communicate with these creatures.

They obviously wished to talk to him, and

found no problem in doing so, but how was he to return the conversation?

He could but try.

He gave a short, sharp laugh, as an experiment, not knowing what to expect. Their own laughter stopped at once, and the Planimal whom Brog had trapped replied, the words slipping easily into Brog's head: "No, we are not afraid, but curious."

He had read the meaning in the sound that Brog had made.

From then on, it was easy. Brog soon got the hang of thinking (instead of speaking) what he wanted to say, and so long as he accompanied it with a laugh sound, the Planimals understood him.

He learned many things from the Planimals, and to Brog that is just what they were, their own name for their species being unpronounceable.

Their powers of instant metamorphosis depended upon contact with the soil, which accounted for the capture of Brog's Planimal.

They wanted to know about Brog and his people, and why he was there amongst them. Did he know why the Light was dying? They talked for many hours before, gradually, as the novelty of Brog wore off, they began to drift away in twos and threes, their spindly legs, jointed only at hip and ankle, giving them a jerky, comical motion which Brog found most endearing.

Finally, only Brog and his friend were left; he had taken a liking to the Stoop, and seemed in no hurry to leave.

The shadows grew long as they talked, and when Brog made his way to his hollow, Planimal accompanied him, riding easily on Brog's broad shoulder.

They fed together on lushbobs and clear spring water, enjoying each other's company, and when Brog finally slid into his hollow, as his instincts told him he must, Planimal stood by the entrance, turned into a flower, and nodded the Blackhours away.

Brog emerged from his hollow on the following Dayspan refreshed but anxious. It had been three spans since Klan had left him, and it seemed to Brog that he had done nothing towards finding the lair of the Drabkeeper.

True, he had searched far, and one span of the three had been spent in his change to adulthood, but time was running out, and this span's Light seemed dimmer than ever.

Planimal was waiting for him as he emerged.

"Greetings, Brog," he chirped, "what does the Dayspan hold for you?"

Brog sighed, and cast his eyes along the distant horizon.

"Your search," said Planimal. "It must go on, am I right?"

Brog nodded. "The Dayspans grow more dim, my friend, my people more weary, I am sure. I must find the one I seek – the Drabkeeper."

"If such a creature lived in these mountains we would know." He cocked his red head on one side. "But I have given it thought." He pointed a spindly finger to two neat, snow-capped peaks in the distance. "In those, the Raa'yun Mountains, we are told, there lives a creature ancient and wise, whose task it is to record all happenings."

Brog's interest showed.

"No one has ever seen him," Planimal continued, "but we have known always that he is there, watching, seeing and recording."

Brog stroked his chin, thoughtfully. "Is it said amongst you that he knows all things?"

Planimal nodded his petalled head. "It is."

"Then I feel he is the one, Planimal. He must be, for amongst the Stoop he is known for the same things. I must approach him."

"It is a long, hard journey, Brog," said Planimal, "but your mind tells me that you are determined."

"It is what I must do," said Brog, simply, already beginning to block up the entrance to his hollow in readiness for leaving.

"You will need a guide," said Planimal.

"I have the mountains in sight, I need only cut a straight path."

Planimal leaned against a rock and crossed his ankles. "Hmmm . . . maybe, maybe not. The Uplands can be dangerous, and if the traveller knows not the danger signs . . ."

He paused, watching for a reaction from Brog, but none was forthcoming.

"As it happens," he continued, "I have nothing of importance to do for a while . . ."

He strolled a few paces, his hands behind his back, feigning nonchalance, but in truth, desperate not to lose, so soon, the friend he had found.

Brog smiled. It would be good to have company. He had grown to like Planimal in the short time he had known him.

"Come, little friend," he said with a grin, "we will travel together."

Planimal's face lit up with delight as Brog swung him to his shoulder.

Brog set his face towards the distant mountains, and with Planimal's chuckles breaking on the crisp morning air, the two friends set off, Brog's strides causing the little creature to jog briskly on his perch.

CHAPTER 5

Frog's steady pace ate up the ground as, with the Glowurld at his back, he strode towards the Raa'yun Mountains, and with each step he took, the hope rose within him that there he would find the one he sought – the Drabkeeper, recorder of all things Drab.

Living side by side with that hope, was the fear that the Drabkeeper might be powerless to intervene; the Elder Stoop at the Council had been adamant that all creatures shaped their own destinies. Perhaps the most he could hope for was advice, but advice from a creature wise enough to oversee the whole Drabworld would be worthy advice indeed.

His desire to avenge the death of his mother was strong within him, as was the urge to help his people fight the Gork, but not for a moment did he consider his journey to be wasted time.

He thought of Pik. Had *he* escaped the Flatplace massacre? And if so, was he now a mature Stoop as Brog was?

And, as always, he thought of Lin, and saw again, in his mind's eye, the two of them sitting on the rock which overlooked the Glowurld as the Dayspan faded.

At such a time, the colours of the sky were beautiful to behold, and he felt again, for a moment, the tranquillity and the happiness he had always felt whenever he was with her.

Planimal, riding easily now on Brog's broad shoulder, proved to be an entertaining companion, and kept up a constant stream of chatter, insistent that he gave Brog not only the complete history of the Uplands, but chapter and verse on how his people came to be there.

In between times, he would point out unusual features of the landscape, and jump up and down excitedly whenever he spotted any of the small animals who lived there – the Dik'laar, the Rag'tun, or the bouncing, nervous, Laa'but.

The ground was rising gradually and becoming more rocky, and Planimal began to grow anxious that, should he need to, he wouldn't be able to find a piece of softground quickly enough upon which to metamorphose into his plant state.

His anxiety showed in a reduction in his chatter, which Brog was not too unhappy about anyway, but when he began to shout, "There! . . . and there!" every time he saw a patch of soil, Brog had to reassure him that, sitting where he was, he was about as safe (and therefore less likely to need to metamorphose) as he had ever been.

They walked for most of that Dayspan, resting once only to nourish themselves, which in Planimal's case consisted of digging his toes into a mossy crevice, but although the valley now below them showed how high and how far they had come, the Raa'yun Mountains appeared to be no nearer.

"Raa'yun," murmured Brog as he eyed the snowy peaks, the meaning of the word in ancient Stooptalk rolling through his mind, " 'Too Far'. A name well fitting."

Planimal didn't answer as he was in a plant-state, but nodded his petalled head in agreement.

Two more hours of walking saw a noticeable

decrease in the Light, and Brog knew the span was coming to an end.

The Source of Light, which from this altitude showed more clearly than just the bright glow on the horizon that he and Klan had seen when they entered the Uplands, had become dim enough to be looked at, and its reflection upon the mountains ahead had given the snow a mellow, golden cast.

It would soon be time to find a hollow, and Brog began to spy out the land as he strode.

Planimal had happily resumed his chatter, and Brog first became aware that something was wrong when the little fellow's voice suddenly faltered and stopped.

In the silence which followed, Brog felt him begin to quake, and felt his shoulder gripped by Planimal's stiffened toes.

Brog stopped abruptly in mid-stride.

An image had flashed into his mind, momentarily, but vivid enough to leave an impression of a cruel, sharp beak fronting black, murderous eyes.

He shook his head to clear the picture that had forced its way onto his subconcious.

Planimal was frozen with fear, and Brog had to ease him gently from his hair, to which he had clung in desperation.

"What is it, little one, what do you fear?"

soothed Brog, scanning the land around for a danger he might not yet have seen.

Again the image welled in his mind: fearful, hooked talons upon powerful, black legs.

Planimal was standing as though mesmerized, and at once Brog knew that the images were coming from him.

It had to be so.

Planimal's fear was being transmitted to Brog's mind, it was an alarm signal, but what had set it off? What had Planimal seen? Heard? Sensed?

Brog set him on the stony ground, and instinctively, his feet scrabbled pitifully for soft earth, and finding none, he flung himself at Brog's leg and clung there in panic.

Brog went down on his other knee, brought Planimal's face close to his.

"Planimal . . . what danger . . . tell me!"

In reply, Planimal raised a quaking arm and pointed a leafy finger at the darkening sky, his eyes wide with terror. Brog searched the heavens, but saw nothing but a flock of distant birds, flapping almost lazily across the void.

Another mental picture from Planimal made him flinch. Oily-black wings pierced his consciousness, and Planimal spoke, his voice cracked with dread.

"Klakkaburds!" he croaked, "Klakkaburds

. . . Klakkaburds!" and he buried his face in Brog's shin.

Brog stood, looked to the flock in the sky, already much nearer, bigger birds than he had first thought, but still winging their way idly enough.

With Planimal clinging leech-like to his leg, Brog strode to a higher rock, the better to see, shading his eyes from the dying glare behind the birds.

As he watched, a startling change came over the flock. Their relaxed flapping became more agitated, and, as a body, almost as though they were joined by invisible wires, they changed direction, swinging left to come in direct line with Brog.

With a speed which seemed hardly credible, they covered the remaining distance, and in what seemed like moments, they were overhead, flying round and round, each behind the other, in one enormous circle.

Brog could see that every eye of the twenty or so huge black creatures was fixed on him, every neck craned in his direction, as the circle in which they flew grew ever smaller. Until now, they had been silent, but first one, and then another began to voice the sound which gave them their name: "Klakaa! . . . Klakkaaa! . . . Klakkaaaaaaa!"

The grating scream echoed across the rocky landscape, filling the air and driving a dread into Brog's very soul. Never had he heard such a truly awful sound. It beat upon the ears, and numbed the senses.

In desperation, Brog sprinted to a fallen tree and broke off a thick branch with a wrench of his powerful shoulders. Nowhere was there any cover, and it was evident that an attack was imminent.

Even as he armed himself, the Klakkaburds fell silent and an ominous quiet, in a way more horrid than the sound itself, wrapped around the two friends.

It was then the Klakkas made their move.

One huge beast broke from the circle, folded its wings, and dived, dropping like a stone. Immediately, the others copied, forming behind the leader in two straight ranks, until the whole flock were in the shape of a "V" which pointed directly at Brog and plummeted at tremendous speed.

Brog braced himself, Planimal clinging tightly around his leg, and lifted the branch in readiness.

The wind whistled through the feathers of the Klakkas as they hurtled to the attack, and Brog kept his eye on the leader, judging the narrowing distance, drawing his striking arm further and further back as it approached. The hooked beak was aimed straight at his throat, the glinting talons grasping for his face as Brog swung the branch with all his might.

The Klakka disintegrated in a flurry of blood and black feathers, but its place was taken at once by the bird immediately behind, and Brog knew he had no time to draw back his club for another blow. Instead, he ducked, and the Klakka shot over his head, skimmed the ground, and tried to rise to rejoin the attack. Had Brog not been busy gauging the approach of the third bird, he would have seen the second bird impale itself on a branch of the fallen tree. With the next Klakka almost upon him, he swung again, and felt the sickening crunch as the branch connected with the bird's head, and the oily, loathsome body dropped at his feet.

This time Brog continued the path of his stroke, and swung in a complete circle, catching the next attacker from an unexpected direction, and sending it whirling and screeching to the ground many lengths away.

So fast were the Klakkas coming in that Brog knew he had no chance of hitting each as it arrived. Sooner or later one would get through, and the others would be on him like a pack of wild Do'gaans. This was obviously the Klakkas' strategy, a suicide attack aimed at overwhelming the victim by weight of numbers.

Brog played his hand well, electing to aim for alternate birds, and to duck and roll in an effort to dodge the ones in between.

The fact that they were evenly spaced in their formation helped him to set up a rhythm, and within the space of ten breaths, the ground became littered with bodies as he struck and weaved and struck again, moving with all the grace and agility of an experienced Stoop-warrior, young as he was.

The first attack ended as the last Klakka skimmed his head, one talon cutting a neat slice in his shoulder before soaring up to join the dozen or so others who had survived his fierce defence, and who were regrouping in a circle above. Again, the dreaded, blood-chilling cry rang through the air: "Klakaaa! . . . Klakkk-aaaaa! . . . Klakkaaaaaaa!"

Brog looked at his bloodstained club, and saw with dismay the crack running its full length. One more blow would split it completely, and without a weapon of some kind, another attack could have only one result.

He ran his eye over the fallen tree; not another branch big enough to use, and already the Klakkaburds were beginning to decrease their flying circle.

Planimal lifted his head from Brog's leg, and gazed around at the bodies in disbelief. Brog smiled at him, mirthlessly, his chest heaving with exertion.

"We cost them dearly, little friend," he said.

"They will attack again?" asked Planimal, stepping cautiously onto the tree trunk.

Brog nodded, indicating his split club. "And we are without a weapon."

"So we die," said Planimal, simply.

"If there was a rockhole . . ." murmured Brog, looking around, but the area offered no refuge whatsoever. Planimal eyed the circling birds and shuddered. ". . . or softground for you."

He knelt and felt the area where the tree had once stood.

"See, Planimal . . . here! Here is softground!"

Planimal ran over, dug his toes in.

"At least you will be safe," urged Brog.

Planimal looked up at him. "We are not a brave people," he said, almost as an apology.

"You are a gentle people," replied Brog, taking his hand, "and this Wurld is in need of gentleness."

Above them, the Klakkaburds cut short their screeching; the attack was about to begin.

Planimal squeezed Brog's hand. "I will never forget Brog the Stoop," he whispered, and a great green tear rolled from his eye.

"Goodbye, little friend," breathed Brog, then he rose, turned, and strode to what they both knew would be certain death.

CHAPTER 6

The egg of a Gork is almost as ugly and menacing as a Gork itself.

Big enough to need two arms to carry, it is roughly round, a dirty yellow-grey in colour, and has a lumpy, pitted shell. The sort of object which would be instinctively avoided by anyone who came across it, even without knowing what it was.

The Gork were hermaphrodites, and therefore capable of reproducing themselves without any mating process, and they revered the egg above all else, indeed it was the one thing in their whole hateful existence which they could be said to care about.

One hundred and fifty-five Gork eggs lay in rows on a bed of dry sponmoss, not five hundred leaps inside the Great Gloom at its border with the Darkness.

The grey, pitiful Light filtered through the trees surrounding the Nesting Station, lending an eerie glow, as a young female Stoop edged along the paths between the eggrows, stopping at each egg to give it the half-turn it needed, to allow what Light there was to fall upon the thin shell. The full-length cloak she wore, hooded over her head against the fine drizzle of rain that was falling, did not conceal the fact that she was quite beautiful, with large, oval eyes and gleaming black hair, which swung as she worked, methodically, without enthusiasm.

The graceful movements which should have accompanied her beauty were hampered by the short length of stranglevine tied from ankle to ankle, which allowed her only to shuffle.

On the perimeter of the Station prowled two NewBreed, sullenly guarding the nest, and growling from time to time at the dozen or so other prisoners, all young females, Stoopettes, as they went mechanically about their duties.

As she turned the eggs, Lin kept a keen eye on the guards, working her way purposefully towards the darker end of the nest, and at the same time, further away from their scrutiny.

The hatred she felt for her captors was kept in check by the desire to live long enough to see them driven back into the Darkness for ever, and above all, she longed to play a part in their downfall.

It was this ambition, to see her people free again, which made her very careful not to anger the Gork unnecessarily, but to do what was expected of her until such time as she could pay them back for the injustices to her people, and the four long Moonruns spent as their slave.

She reached and felt the barkneedle in her pocket.

Each egg she turned brought her nearer to the end of the eggrow, and soon she would be in the darkest part of the nest, away from the prying eyes of the guards.

Not a Dayspan went by which was not filled with thoughts of the people she had known before her capture: her mother, Plin, her good friend Pik and, of course, Brog.

Most of her thoughts were of Brog.

If only she could be sure that they knew she was still alive.

If only she knew *they* were still alive.

The Nesting Station lay by the Way which leads to the Darkness, and had been set up many Moonruns before the great ground-shake which had dimmed the Light, for the Gork had been planning the NewBreed for a long time, anticipating the day when they would be free from the restrictions of darkness, free to invade and rule the whole Terrawurld. The great ground-shake had brought the possibility of that day much nearer, enabling them to make their first Lightime raids.

Lin and the other prisoners had seen the Gork return from their attack on the Flatplace, roaring and screaming, swaggering triumphantly, with Redeye their Leader carried high.

Afterwards, the guards had mocked them, taunted them, acted out their killings over and over again for their own amusement.

Each prisoner knew that their loved ones would have been at the Flatplace that day, and each could only hope that their families had survived.

So, the Stoopettes had kept their dignity, had not given the Gork the satisfaction of seeing how anxious they felt.

Only two spans ago, they had heard the dying screams of a Gork further along the Way, and knew that the Stoopwarriors were beginning to fight back. They too had to live to fight another day, and as prisoners – especially as prisoners working with eggs – there were, well, 'certain things' they could do to prevent the Gork from having it all their own way.

Lin turned the last egg in the row and reached cautiously for the barkneedle in her pocket. One stab through the shell would be enough to break the airseal; the tiny hole left would be undetectable, and one more egg would remain unhatched. In this way, Lin and her friends had accounted for the destruction of one egg in every five (a failure rate which the Gork had come to accept as normal) without arousing suspicion.

"Lin!"

She started as she heard the whisper of her name, and turned to see her friend shuffling towards her, pretending to be checking the eggs in another row.

Swiftly, Lin applied the barkneedle, heard the faint hiss of escaping air, and turned to Kora.

"Lin, I have news."

Of all the prisoners, Kora had been there the longest. Kora it was who could understand the guttural growltalk of the Gork without them suspecting that she could. It was through Kora that the others knew what little they did about what had been happening in the Great Gloom since their capture.

"Tell me," urged Lin, as they both busied themselves for the benefit of the watching guards.

Kora spoke low, her face turned away.

"The Gork will attack the Sheerstone!"

"I believe it not!"

"Even now, they march."

"Not the Sheerstone! Not the Gork! It is not their way!"

"I can tell only what I have heard," hissed Kora.

Lin caught her eye. "Then there is more to hear, I know it! Come, we must talk."

Even as they moved off, one of the guards, noticing them in the shadows, growled a warning and moved a step towards them, returning to his position only when he saw that they had separated.

Lin and Kora made their way to the hut in which the prisoners rested, and once inside, set to in earnest conversation.

Kora had overheard the guards talking.

The main body of the Gork army was expected to pass in one hour's time, and she was adamant that they were on their way to the Sheerstone.

"I doubt not what you heard," said Lin, "but I feel something is wrong."

Kora frowned, puzzled.

"Kora!" Lin was exasperated with her friend. "You know as well as I that the Gork attack only the weak and defenceless, as at the Flatplace.

The Sheerstone is easy to defend, our people must be strong there, well armed. It makes not sense!"

"Perhaps Redeye is becoming bold, convinced he is strong enough to do it?"

"Redeye is no fool. No, rather I think, he has some other plan hiding behind this one."

"What could it be?"

"That we must discover."

"But the guards talk only of the attack on the Sheerstone, anything else I would have heard," insisted Kora.

"Then we must discover from Redeye himself," said Lin, thoughtfully.

Kora would have pressed her further, but Lin laid a hand on her arm as to their ears came the sound of many clawed feet stomping along the Way, and the unmistakable drag of many tails.

"It has begun," Kora muttered grimly.

"As has our chance to help our people," put in Lin.

"In what way?"

Lin moved to the door of the hut and peered at the first of the Gork legions trooping past not twenty leaps away.

"We must find the real reason behind what Redeye is doing. Attack the Sheerstone he may, but I fear it will be only to hide his true purpose."

"You have a plan." It was a statement, not a question.

Lin nodded. "To join the march!"

Kora gasped, mouth open. "What?"

"Are you with me?"

A little under an hour later the two friends were hidden in bush by the side of the Way.

A constant stream of Gork continued to rumble past them, singly, in pairs, and in groups, varying in size and in bulk, but all with the white stripe of the NewBreed across their face, all heavily armed with spikeballs and four-bladed spears.

Redeye's arrival was heralded by the grunts in unison of the ten bearers of his platform, five front and five back, whose muscles shone with the oils secreted by their efforts, as they bore their Leader waist-high and defiantly.

Redeye sat, an immense figure, cross-legged, his tail wrapped around his waist, the chest scales reflecting opalescent colour, the glittering orbs that gave him his name burning in his head, lips drawn back in a permanent snarl, and the blood of Lin and Kora ran cold as they saw him.

Following the platform came a pitiful sight of some sixteen female Stoop prisoners, slaves to the needs of Redeye, roped in twos, and stumbling to keep up with the procession, knowing that if they were to fall, the rest of the Gork following on would have no hesitation in trampling them into the ground.

Two, in fact, did fall as they passed the bush behind which the friends were crouched. Brought down by a swift tug of the vine around their ankles, they lay, grateful if surprised, out of sight, whilst their places were taken by Lin and Kora.

So swiftly did it happen that not a Gork noticed, and the whole procession went on its way, little knowing that, in the midst of all their might, a tiny seed of destruction had just been planted.

CHAPTER 7

Frog's thoughts were clear and his mind calm, as the Klakkaburds hurtled towards him from a darkening sky.

If he had to die, so be it, but he would die fighting.

The thought of the way he had panicked and run from the Flatplace still burned in his memory; this time he would stand and die like a Stoopwarrior.

He felt anger that this should happen before he had had time to prove himself, and the faces of the people he had failed leapt into his mind:

Lin – now he would not be able to fulfil his promise to rescue her.

Klan – who had put so much trust in him to find the Drabkeeper.

His mother – she had given her life that he might live, but for what? To die a forgotten death on a barren mountain top?

He had failed them all, but at least this moment would be a glorious one; he was determined that his death would be the one thing they could be proud of.

He spread his feet, braced himself, and prepared to sell his life dearly, swallowing the bitter disappointment of having been so close to the Drabkeeper, and yet, so far.

In the softground by the fallen tree, Planimal, in a half-plant state, watched heartbroken as his friend faced a savage death with his head held high.

Such bravery he had never seen, or even heard of. Here on the Uplands, there were only two creature-types, the killer and the victim, the strong and the weak. If the weak did not outsmart the strong, he became the victim, this was accepted – even by the victim himself.

Never had he seen one like Brog, a victim about to fight for his life.

The Klakkas came in at an angle, the leading bird already grasping greedily with its huge claws. All that Brog could hope to do was protect his eyes for as long as possible.

Whilst he could see, he could defend himself.

He realized, also, the importance of remaining on his feet for as long as he could, for once he fell, they would swarm all over him, pecking, raking, stabbing.

At that moment, Brog would willingly have traded half his life for a good Magnawood Ka'thuk.

He felt a movement by his leg.

Glancing down, he saw that Planimal had left the safety of his softground, and running across, had wrapped himself around Brog's shin, where he now clung, looking up at Brog with total trust on his flower-like face.

With the Klakkaburds almost upon them, Brog felt a surge of warmth and gratitude for the tiny plant-animal who had sacrificed his own safety so that Brog might not die alone.

Planimal's brave action, made braver by the fact that he was a naturally timid creature, gave Brog new strength, and he awaited the arrival of the winged killers almost eagerly.

The rush of wind through those oily, black feathers grew to a roar as, feet first, talons glinting, the lead bird reached for Brog's throat.

Brog stretched, intending to grasp the thick ankle and dash the bird to the ground, but at that very moment of contact, the strangest of things happened.

The screeching, the wind noise, in fact *all* noise ceased as suddenly as if a door had been closed. Planimal looked up, startled to see the bird that only a microsecond ago was about to rip at Brog, crumple and collapse as though it had run into a brick wall.

Brog could not believe his eyes as two, three, four Klakkas broke their necks in full flight against what appeared to be an invisible barrier between him and them.

He reached upwards, and his fingers came into contact with a smooth, curved surface, and followed the curve down and around to his feet.

"Planimal . . ." he murmured incredulously, "something surrounds us!"

Planimal felt for himself, and gave an "Ooooh" of complete astonishment.

The remaining Klakkaburds wheeled and fluttered around them, angry, puzzled, unwilling to commit themselves to an attack which could not be carried through.

As far as Brog could make out, they were encased in a giant bubble, firm enough to the touch, but invisible to the eye, though marks made by the Klakkas who had perished running into its surface were clear to be seen.

With a lurch which almost threw them off their feet, the bubble began to rise, taking them with it. Planimal ran up onto Brog's shoulder, whilst Brog wrestled with the sensation of floating in air.

All he could do was brace his arms with the palms of his hands pressed against the walls of the bubble, his feet spread, in an effort to keep his balance.

Planimal chattered with excitement as the bubble rose higher, leaving behind the broken bodies of the killer birds to be eaten by the survivors, and drifted out across the Uplands in the direction of the Raa'yun Mountains.

Just what was happening, and why, Brog could only guess. His hopes told him to believe this was the Drabkeeper's work, but his senses told him no.

As they drifted smoothly over the land, rising steadily higher, he gradually relaxed his pressure on the walls of the bubble, and crouched, eventually coming to sit cross-legged in the centre, gazing around him in absolute wonder, Planimal perched now on his head, now on his knee.

So high were they now that Planimal was able to point out their point of origin, his homeland. Off to the right, the plains of the Glowurld spread to the mountains of the horizon, feature-less except for the occasional disc-like hollow, and Brog wondered aloud what sort of creatures the Glowurld might be home to.

Still bright on the horizon due to their height, stood the Source of Light, its shape indistinct.

"There!" cried Brog, pointing, and far below, catching the last dying gleam from the source, lay the Great Gloom, with its Treelands getting more and more dense as it neared that black and evil area, the Darkness.

"Your home," chirped Planimal.

Brog nodded. He could make out the Flatplace, and the thought of his Mother cut like a knife.

Rising to poke its head from the foliage was the massive Sheerstone.

If the Stoop had retreated there, there was still a chance.

Before very long, it became obvious to the two friends that they were indeed on a direct course to the Raa'yun Mountains. Their peaks, much closer now, they could see to be but two high points in a chain of mountains which ran in a circle, and if the bubble kept to its path, they would pass between them.

Exactly that happened, and within no more than a hundred heartbeats, the left peak sailed majestically past their line of vision, the crisp white snow like a sheet dropped over the mountain top.

Almost at once, the bubble began to drop

slowly, their speed checked to a crawl, and looking down they saw that they were entering what appeared to be a crater.

Already they were below the rim, and although the mountains blocked the Light from the Source as they dropped even lower, the crater valley into which they were drifting seemed to give off a glow of its own from below.

Helpless to do anything but watch and wait, they scanned the crater walls for something, anything, that might give a clue as to why they had been brought here.

The bubble had done a complete circuit of the inside of the crater when they noticed, for the first time, two small platforms jutting out from the wall maybe fifty leaps apart.

It became apparent that they were headed for one or other of the platforms. Indeed, the bubble seemed unable to make up its mind, and swung indecisively back and forth between the two, hovering first over one, then the other.

Eventually, with the slightest of bumps, they came down upon one of them, and at once the waft of a breeze and the stillness which followed their landing told them, even before they reached out to feel, that their transport had evaporated as quickly and as mysteriously as it had appeared.

They were standing on the platform of stone,

surrounded on three sides by an immense drop to the crater floor, and faced with nothing but the sheer, blank wall which soared many hundreds of lengths above them.

Planimal lay flat and peered over the platform's edge, giving an "Ooooohh!" which echoed eerily around the huge crater, his eyes wide with the wonder of it all.

Brog reviewed their situation. They were stranded, no way up, down, or off the platform. But he had arrived at his goal, of that he was sure. By now, they would both have had their bones picked clean by the Klakkas.

The grating sound startled them, and its echo around the crater walls disguised its origin, until they turned and saw that a curved section of the wall behind them had swung inwards, revealing a passage into the mountain.

Without alternatives to choose from, Brog, with only a moment's hesitation, swung Planimal onto his shoulder and ducked cautiously beneath the opening and into the passage.

The walls inside were ice-smooth, and led, they could see at once, in a perfectly straight line to a large blue door maybe ten strides away.

It took less than ten of Brog's strides to get there, and after four, the opening in the rock behind them swung closed with a soft but definite thud.

Once again, they had no choice but to take the only option available – the blue door.

It had no handle, but when Brog pushed lightly on one side of it, the door swung open easily.

The room beyond was dark and quiet.

Brog lowered Planimal to the ground and peered warily inside before stepping tenderly over the threshold.

The moment he did so, the room was lit with a glow only slightly below Brog's sight-pain threshold. Indeed, he had to reduce his eye size quickly to compensate for it.

As his vision clarified, he gasped at what he saw.

Bathed in the glow of the room, snarling and menacing, stood the figure of the most hated creature he knew – Redeye the Gork!

Planimal stood petrified, toes scrabbling on the smooth floor.

Brog's heart thudded against his ribs, the shock of being confronted by his enemy subsiding slowly, to be replaced by the hatred and loathing he felt for the black-hearted animal that had slain his Mother and brought such misery to the Stoop nation.

But why here? What exactly was Redeye doing here?

Without a weapon of any kind, Brog, for the

second time that day, knew that he was facing impossible odds, but without means of escape, he also knew that he had no choice but to fight.

Without another thought, he gathered his strength and, spurred on by his hatred, he launched himself at the gloating, saliva-dripping monster.

With little hope of actually reaching his target, Brog nevertheless went straight for Redeye's throat, only to find that he was clawing at empty air. He landed on all fours, rolled, and was on his feet again in a flash, his back to the wall, casting wildly about the small room for his adversary. Whichever way he looked, Redeye was nowhere to be seen – he had simply vanished.

Brog blinked in disbelief, doubting his sanity for a brief moment, then a movement caught his eye, and there was Planimal, peering, boggle-eyed, around the doorway.

"Klakkaburd?" he asked, a distinct question in his voice.

Brog shot him a puzzled look.

"Where is Klakkaburd?" continued Planimal.

"Redeye was here . . ." panted Brog.

Planimal shook a leafy head, stepped inside the room, gazing into every corner.

"No," he chattered, his little arms trembling, "it was Klakkaburd."

Brog rubbed a hand thoughtfully over his chin. Whatever each of them had seen, the room was now quite empty.

CHAPTER 8

Deep inside the Sheerstone, where the tunnels opened up into the widest rockhole, a wartalk was taking place.

Around the flatrock which served as a table, flecked with yellow light from the torchflames set high on the rough walls, sat the lesser Stooplords, Marshals, and Stoopwarriors Supreme, and at the head of the table sat Klan the Golden, his huge scarred hands, witness to a thousand battles, resting on the arms of the Council Chair that had been fashioned for him.

Composed, he listened now to an account of the current standing of the Stoop nation being delivered by a Vice-Marshal, and as he listened, his expression, along with that of the others who heard, grew grim.

He heard how almost a quarter of all Stoops living in the Great Gloom had been killed, either in the Flatplace massacre, or in clashes with the Gork since then.

Although the raiding parties of young Stoop-warriors were having some success, their effectiveness was being hampered, since they also had to provide protection for the groups of food-gatherers who had to go out daily from the Sheerstone to collect berries, fish, and culweed.

The Gork seemed to be everywhere, and the general opinion was that they were reproducing themselves far faster than they could be killed.

The speaker sat, and an ominous silence ran around the gathering; eyes met and heads shook in a torrent of unspoken fears and regrets. Each knew the seriousness of the position, just as they knew that Klan would now be looking to them for solutions to their problems.

Dork indicated that he had something to say, and a nod from Klan brought him swiftly to his feet, a determined scowl on his face.

"Our survival," he began, "depends on our ability to kill Gork."

Nods of agreement.

"Within the Sheerstone we are safe, though

we live as scutterbeetles, but whilst we cower safely ..." (the word was spat out with contempt) "whilst we *cower*, the Gork become stronger and multiply."

Palms were slapped repeatedly against battle-wood in support. Dork raised a hand and continued as the noise abated.

"It is to the Nestings of the NewBreed that we must turn our attention. Whilst a Gork egg remains, we will never be free. We must find the Nestings and destroy them!"

There were many who agreed with him, and he sat to a chorus of approval. Another sought Klan's permission, and stood, all eyes went to him.

"Dork speaks wisely, the Nestings should be found and destroyed, but even so, this would not solve our problem. Already there are enough Gork to plague our people for many Moon-runs to come, and remember that they have the Lighthours now. Gone is the time when we needed only to fear them in the Blacktime."

"Attack the Nestings now!" someone called.

"Hah! Find them first!" was the sceptical reply.

"The Nestings are no danger," cried a warrior, leaping to his feet and forgetting the permission he needed to do so: "An egg did not kill my father! A Gork did! We must attack the Gork!"

Everyone present wanted a say, and the comments flew like leaves in a wind, anger rising steadily.

Klan watched it all stoically, knowing his warriors needed a chance to vent their anger and frustration; at some time during this meeting, at a moment he would choose, he would reveal the involvement of Brog in the scheme of things, but first he wanted to hear what his commanders had to suggest.

The only other person unmoved by the argument that was taking place was the Elder, Goth; he watched as the tension grew, one knowing eye on Klan, and at the height of the noise, upon a brief nod from his Stooplord, he lifted his sword and brought it crashing down flat on the table.

The effect was magical.

Shouts ceased abruptly, all heads turned his way as, with an imperceptible nod of acknowledgement to Klan, he rose slowly to his feet.

The aggression dissipated, Stoop slumped back in their seats, muttering.

Goth took his time, looked around at each face.

"Egg or Gork?" he postured. "Which to kill first? One thing is sure, none of us will live to see the last one destroyed, for there are too many, and more by the Dayspan."

Their faces reflected the grimness of this truth.

"I spoke at the Flatplace, on the day of the great killing, I spoke of the Light. I say again – it is the return of the Light, and *only* the return of the Light that will rid us of the Gork, yes, even the NewBreed, for our normal levels of Light would be fatal to them, I doubt it not!"

"And how would we return the Light, old Stoop? Or would you have us *ask* it to shine more brightly?"

Goth took no offence, simply smiled and looked directly to Klan.

"Not I," Goth said.

The others followed his gaze.

Klan stared back at them for a long moment, his steely eyes resting briefly upon each one in turn.

His voice was one of calm, reason, and authority, and as usual when he spoke, everyone listened.

They listened as he explained his swift departure from the battlefield at the Flatplace, and there were looks of surprise as he revealed for the first time that Brog was his son. He told them of the journey they had both made to the Uplands, and all the time, those of the Council listened intently, the knowledge growing inside them that their best hope might indeed be in the plan that their Stooplord had already put into action – even while they were arguing about what the next step might be.

When Klan had finished, the atmosphere in the room was much more subdued. Speculation led to questions, and doubts arose regarding the mythical Drabkeeper whom most saw as a creature only from ancient legend.

Dork it was who pointed out that even if the Drabkeeper did exist, the mission to contact him was not a job for a Stoopling, even a Royal Stoopling such as Brog.

"Brog believes, as I do, that the Drabkeeper lives," explained Klan, "therefore, he seeks one who exists. Another, less believing, would be searching for an uncertainty, and would soon convince themselves that their search was in vain."

"But . . . such a difficult search . . . by one so young. . . ?"

Goth rose again. "What has age to do with the issue?" he said. "It is the determination, the belief, and the commitment that matter. We are fortunate that in Brog, son of Klan, we have all these."

Dork gazed around the faces of his followers, and saw in them the hope that wasn't there at the start of this wartalk. He came slowly to his feet, facing Klan.

"If the Drabkeeper lives, he *must* be found," he conceded.

"The Drabkeeper lives," returned Klan, "and my son will find him."

CHAPTER 9

The plat! plat! of Brog's bare feet resounded from the walls as he padded endlessly and uneasily around the room in which he and Planimal found themselves trapped.

The blue door through which they had entered had closed firmly, and Brog had inspected the walls twice and found not the slightest sign of an opening, gap, or crack anywhere.

Still unexplained was the mysterious vision of Redeye, which Planimal had seen as a Klakka-burd, as they had entered. Now, as Brog rested on his haunches, and Planimal strode jerkily over, he could feel the frustration of being trapped beginning to rise in him.

"Why does he keep us here?" he muttered angrily. "Where is he?"

"All around," said Planimal, with such certainty that Brog knew it was true. "I feel it."

Brog stood, anger beginning to show.

"Then let him show himself!" he said aloud, and swung round, startled, as a high-pitched voice behind him replied on the instant.

"You're quite right, quite right of course, it is about time I introduced myself, only you can't be too careful, can you?"

The room had suddenly become much longer, and from round the corner of that part of the room which had most definitely not been there a few moments ago, drifted the strangest figure that either Brog or Planimal had ever seen.

'Drifted' *was* the right word, for there was no movement of the lower part of the strange body which was gliding swiftly towards them, except for four round, black discs, seemingly one at each corner of the person, which rolled him forward.

He was small but bulky, with two blue eyes, ears one on either side of the face (unlike Brog's which were set higher on his head), and a tuft of yellow hair.

Brog was unsure whether it was clothes he was wearing, or if what he had on was actually him, and if it was, then he was red from waist to neck, with a cluster of spotty material beneath his chin, whilst from the waist down he was bright, shiny, and extremely spindly, right down to the black discs which rolled round and round as he moved.

He came to a silent stop, and to the friends' amazement, unfolded two red legs from underneath himself, became separated from the shiny bit, and stepped forward with a huge smile on his face, to show a row of even, white teeth.

"So pleased to meet you," fluted the Drabkeeper, clasping a long black stick with a shiny top, "Brog, isn't it? And the friend you call Planimal?"

Brog gaped at the creature whose head came on a level with his chest. That he was friendly there could be no doubt for, strange as his face was, with no snout, and such a small mouth, it was clearly a face empty of threat, and Brog's anger at being imprisoned began to drain from him.

"I don't mind if you stare," went on the Drabkeeper in his peculiar, piping voice. "Please feel free to stare all you like. You will not have seen a creature like me before, of that I have no doubt."

"*You* are the Drabkeeper?" murmured Brog, wondering why he should feel a sense of disappointment. Perhaps it was because he had built up an impression in his mind of what the

Drabkeeper should look like. Surely one so powerful and legendary should look, well, just a *little* more awesome than this?

The stories passed down the years had made no mention of a short, brightly dressed, ordinary-looking creature with a skin the colour of Brog's own tongue!

"I am a Human," he said, "well . . . Human-ish," and smiled even wider. "Do sit down, make yourselves comfortable."

With that, he twisted the shiny knob of his black stick, and three hexagonal sections of the floor arose on columns. The Drabkeeper perched on one, leaving his guests to do the same on the others.

"I must first of all apologize for your fright as you arrived," he said, "a little test we have to do, I'm afraid. Your worst fear is picked from your mind and, well, brought to life."

He leaned forward, as though only they should hear.

"Supposed to give a final insight into the kind of spirit you have."

"And what kind of 'spirits' have we?" said Brog, unimpressed that they should have been put to any kind of test, particularly one of that nature.

The Drabkeeper looked suitably sorry for his actions.

"You're the only creatures to have reached here in over two thousand Lightyears, maybe that answers your question."

It didn't, and Brog said so.

"I'm not exactly easy to get at, you may have noticed. Can't just drop in any old time. I don't think you realize just how well you did in getting here."

"But you brought us . . ." Brog began.

"Oh no," interjected the Drabkeeper, and spread his palms to emphasize the point. "Your belief brought you. You see, even at the point of death, your belief in my existence was stronger than the fear of dying . . ."

Brog frowned his bewilderment, and the Drabkeeper went on: "Doesn't happen very often. That belief, and your resolve, and your love of justice, they all surrounded you at just the right moment. No, it all came from you, young Brog, from your brave heart, not from me."

Brog still looked puzzled.

"I can show you the rule if you like," the Drabkeeper assured him, "I've got it written down somewhere . . ."

As he made a move to leave the room, Brog spoke, restraining him. "Please . . . I need your help."

The Drabkeeper hesitated, returned to his

seat, and gave another twist of his stick. A section of floor rose between them, and as it came to a halt, three liquid-filled beakers rose from its flat surface with a suddenness which brought an involuntary "Ooohh" from Planimal, and caused Brog to bob his head in wonder. The contents of the beakers proved so refreshing and satisfying that Brog's apprehension lessened considerably.

He began to throw his questions like verbal rocks, eager for any information which might help his people.

The Drabkeeper listened for no longer than it took to drain his beaker, then held up his five-fingered hands in submission.

"Before you go further, young Brog, you need to know that my power to help is limited. If you'll listen, I'll explain."

And explain he did.

His functions were indeed limited – to a recording of events, and the order of the natural elements within the Drabwurld. Brog learned there was also a Glokeeper to oversee the Glowurld in roughly the same way, but all creatures had, indeed, to shape their own destiny.

For three thousand Lightyears he had watched the creatures of the Drabwurld develop, prevented from interfering by Terrawurld law, and particularly by the all-important Rule of Destiny, isolated from others of his race who populated the Glowurld – the price he had to pay for being granted a deathless existence.

"I volunteered for the job, so I mustn't grumble," he quipped.

'Volunteered' wasn't quite the right word as it turned out. Each and every five thousand Light-years, the Drabkeeper was changed, and the new one chosen from Humans whose lives had been spent assisting the more powerful Glokeeper.

"Always a Human?" Brog wanted to know.

"To become a Drabkeeper, we must exchange our spirits for ones which will last for the next five thousand Lightyears. To do this, we must travel beyond the Source of Light to the brighter Ka region. Humans are the only creatures whose eyes can cope with that." He shrugged. "Sorry. Maybe when Stoop sight has developed further . . ."

Planimal lay across his seat, resting his head in his hand, relaxed, watching their exchange, his head flicking from one to the other as they spoke, like a spectator at a tennis match.

Brog could sense the Drabkeeper's concern for the sickness of the Light, but began to wonder just how much help he could expect in view of the limits to his powers.

The Drabkeeper settled in his seat, one leg dangling loosely over the other.

"I knew someone would come sooner or later," he said, "whether it would be a Stoop, or a Human, or even a Gork, I wasn't sure, just so long as their reason for coming here was a concern for how we all might survive."

"No Gork would care," growled Brog.

"No, no, I do realize what they're like. No manners, no manners at all." He smiled. "I do like a person with nice manners."

Whatever 'manners' were, Brog felt sure they couldn't help him in his quest. The Drabkeeper looked shocked at such a thought.

"Oh, but there you're wrong, young Brog. Good manners and right-thinking go together. 'No manners – no chance', I always say. Oh yes, your good manners have brought you this far, young Brog, and will take you further."

With that, he twisted the knob of his stick once more.

Before them, floating about knee height, unfolded a replica of the whole Terrawurld. Brog and Planimal watched in wonder as the Glowurld and the Drabwurld spread out before them in miniature.

Just as they had done in the floating bubble, they looked down on the Great Gloom, saw the Uplands, the Raa'yun Mountains, the Darkness, everything, in minute detail.

"You see, I *can* suggest how you might tackle

the problem," said the Drabkeeper, and he pointed with his stick to the bright spot on the far side of the Glowurld.

"The Source of Light has burned eternal for as long as the Terrawurld has existed," he said. "Now, it has a fault. How serious it is I cannot tell, but it has to be repaired."

He leaned forward again, eyebrows raised. "Like to try?" The slightest of pauses, then, "Of course you would! Because if you don't – pop! – we all perish, all except the Gork, of course."

The question of whether or not he should make the journey simply didn't occur to Brog.

"How might I get there?"

He used the stick as a pointer. "You must travel from the Great Gloom's edge, across the whole Glowurld, to the Mountains of Separation."

As the Drabkeeper detailed the journey that would have to be made, neither he nor Brog noticed the sadness that had begun to creep over Planimal's face, a sadness he was careful to hide as Brog glanced his way.

"Beyond the Mountains of Separation lies the Valley of Light. There you will find the Mound of Extremes and there, in the centre of the Mound of Extremes, stands the Source."

Brog studied the route for a long moment.

"What dangers?" he asked.

"Oh, hundreds!" chortled the Drabkeeper, and he clapped his hands in joy. "But wouldn't it be absolutely boring if there weren't any? Boring for you, boring for me, because I'll have to watch how you get on – on this thing. Can't help you, as I've said, but I can give you one or two tips."

By the time Brog discovered that 'tips' were not things with which he might defend himself, the Drabkeeper had outlined a number of points for him.

He reserved one point until last.

"Here," he pointed, "in the very centre of the Glowurld, is the Glokeeper's castle."

A note of reverence had crept into his tone.

"The Glokeeper is the very centre of all that is Great and Good in the Terrawurld. His being has shaped all existence for ten thousand Light-years, and his powers come from Ka."

"Ka?"

"Ka is The Eternal."

And no matter how Brog tried, the Drabkeeper would not (or could not) tell more.

"Could not a creature so powerful repair the Light Source?" Brog was compelled to ask.

"If he did, what purpose is our prime rule – the Rule of Destiny? Creatures of the Terrawurld have to rely upon themselves, upon each other, not upon a greater being."

Brog could see the sense in that. Only by solving their own problems could creatures (Drab or Glo) gain any kind of independence.

"You must visit the Glokeeper," he burbled. "He can point out the safest way. Oh, and, would you do me a favour? Would you remind him that he still owes me three beautiful thoughts which I lent to him . . . ooh . . . seventy Lightyears ago."

He tapped the stick on the floor, and immediately the vision disappeared, and there, lying on the table which had held the beakers, was an item. It was a curve of black, shiny substance.

"Shouldn't give you this, really, but I like your face."

It was, he explained, an eyeshield, which, as he got nearer to the Source of Light, he might need.

Brog tucked it into his belt, grateful for the gift.

With a sudden leap, the Drabkeeper sprang to his feet.

"And now, my friends, time to go," he beamed, and spread his arms wide in a gesture which said, as well as any words could, "that's all I can do."

Brog knew that the rest was now up to him.

"You'll be pleased to know, by the way, that

your achievement in getting this far wins you a free ride to the start of your journey, which, in your case, Brog, is to the edge of the Glowurld."

"And my friend?" asked Brog.

The Drabkeeper made no answer, but his face clouded, and he laid a hand on Brog's shoulder.

"The friendship you have, will always be – that I can tell you. And remember, Brog, there is no danger, no enemy, that cannot be overcome by honesty. The sickness of the Light can be cured by one brave heart."

It was perhaps the only note of seriousness that the jovial Drabkeeper had touched upon in the whole course of their conversation and, leaving his words hanging in the air, he climbed aboard his spindly vehicle, and started to glide backwards down the room.

"Goodbye," he squeaked, "good luck, and . . ." here he lifted the tuft of yellow hair on his head in a salute ". . . good day."

Silently, he turned the corner, the last thing in sight being the ends of his fingers which he twiddled in a goodbye wave. The room became shorter, and at the same time the blue door through which they had entered swung wide.

It was while they were standing on the ledge overlooking the drop to the floor of the crater below, that Planimal broke the silence he had kept since the appearance of the Drabkeeper.

"This quest is yours alone, Brog," he told his friend.

"Not so," said Brog. "We found the Drabkeeper together, the danger which threatens my people will soon threaten yours; my fight is your fight, and the journey to the Source of Light will be ours, we will make it together."

With a faint hiss, they felt themselves surrounded by the bubble, and almost in the same moment they were lifted into the air as it took them from the Drabkeeper's lair.

Planimal had grown silent again.

He sat on the floor of the bubble, his limbs drooping, his head bent, and Brog knew there was something wrong.

He knelt and took Planimal's leafy hand. Planimal looked up into Brog's face and saw the unspoken question there. He heaved a sigh, and spoke: "I cannot journey with you across the Glowurld, Brog."

"But why? With me you will be safe."

"You do not understand . . . the Glowurld is of stone, without softground."

Brog's heart suddenly felt very heavy.

What Planimal said was true, and long before they reached the Source, he would be dead from hunger.

"You must go alone."

And with those words, both realized that the time had come to part.

The bubble had, by now, risen from the crater, and was hovering, moving neither one way nor the other. To their right lay the Uplands and Planimal's home, to their left, the Great Gloom.

Suddenly, and quite silently, the floor of the bubble rose and closed around Planimal, encasing him in his own little bubble attached to the outside of Brog's larger one.

Brog clawed at the walls, trying desperately to reintroduce the bubble which surrounded his friend into his own, caring little for any risks he might be taking in doing so.

Why this had happened he didn't know, but all he wanted was to be re-united with the little creature he had grown so fond of and who had shared the dangers of his journey with him.

Planimal seemed to be accepting what was happening to him, almost as though he knew it had to be so, almost as if he knew that what was about to happen was inevitable. He raised a little hand and waved it at Brog in a fond farewell, the tears brimming in his eyes, the little fingers trembling, as his bubble detached itself from the main one and began to drift away on its own.

"My thoughts will be ever with you, Brog," he whispered.

"Planimal!" shouted Brog, "Planimal!" and beat his fists against the bubble's walls.

Planimal smiled a sad smile. His bubble was drifting in the direction of the Uplands.

"We will meet again, little one," called Brog, "I promise you!"

He watched Planimal's bubble until it was a speck in the distance, and hardly noticed that he himself was drifting inexorably in the direction of the Great Gloom and the Glowurld borderland.

CHAPTER 10

Every Stoop's natural instinct is to spend the hours of each Blacktime in a covered hollow, and the ground through which the thick roots of the Rocktree grows is ideal, for there the soil is dry and warm, easy to dig, and the roots provide a structure which is difficult for a predator to penetrate.

Travelling Stoop would make sure that at the end of every Dayspan they found a suitable tree to dig beneath, or maybe an old, unused hollow. Failing that, a rockhole, or even a crevice would suffice.

The need to be safe in the Blacktime was one of those vital instincts born with the Stoop, and came as naturally to them as feeding or breathing.

The instincts of Lin, Kora, and all other female Stoop prisoners were given no such consideration by their captors. As the first few feeble rays of the new span crept through the trees, the Gork guard kicked Lin and Kora from their regeneration trance in the open clearing where they had spent the Blackhours with the other prisoners.

It was the start of a new day, and the mighty Redeye was anxious to march further on his advance towards the Sheerstone.

As the Gork army encampment began to stir and prepare for the trek, the Stoop prisoners were bullied into action, and forced to the task of attending to their Leader's early-morning needs.

As the Stoopettes shuffled around the glade, some collecting food, others preparing water for Redeye to bathe, some laying out his armour and weapons, all talk was of the strange creature who had arrived the previous evening. None had seen a creature like him before, and Lin felt instinctively that his visit to Redeye was an event which could not, somehow, bode well for her people.

It was nothing in the creature's appearance that had caused her to shudder, not his five-fingered hands, nor his smooth coral-coloured skin, or even his tiny, shifty eyes, but the way he moved, not with a stride and an upright back, but with a creeping shuffle, shoulders hunched, eyes constantly darting around him.

He reminded her of a Furro'snake creeping up on a helpless Lopfur.

Kora had been listening to the guards again, and her news was that the creature was a Human, and known as Ju'dal. As had been suspected, he was from the Glowurld.

"Why would Redeye need a visit from a Human if his plan is to attack the Sheerstone?" Kora mused. "What use could Ju'dal be to the Gork? That is what we must find out. He must have something to offer Redeye, something of value, or Redeye would not have dealings with him. "But what?" She spat on the berries she was collecting in the certain knowledge that they would be a part of Redeye's breakfast within the hour.

Lin worked in silence, her thoughts racing.

"Information!" she said, finally. "Who would know more about the Glowurld than a Human?"

"But . . . why should the Glowurld interest Redeye?"

"Don't you see?" urged Lin. "The Light is of

the Glowurld! It is of the Light and its workings he seeks to know!" Realization began to dawn on Kora's honest face. "Redeye wants the sickness to continue, to get worse!"

"But the Humans of the Glowurld, they must want the Light to return, is it not their Wurld also?"

Lin tossed a ball of beetledung into the basket of lushbobs.

"I think that Ju'dal does not speak for all Humans – Ju'dal speaks for himself."

On a high, flat hill overlooking the Gork encampment, Pik and a raiding party of twenty young Stoopwarriors lay flat and peered over the edge of the rise.

They had spotted the Gork army at first Light, and already a messenger was speeding on his way to alert Klan at the Sheerstone.

Pik knew that his twenty Stoop, however brave, would have little effect on a force of several hundred Gork, but he also knew where his duty lay. If he allowed the Gork to march uninterrupted, on their present course they would be at the Sheerstone in two hours. His messenger needed time to get there, Klan needed time to prepare for an attack, though the very idea of the Gork attacking a stronghold did not seem to ring true.

Pik and his troops were going to have to delay the Gork march.

Lin and Kora, a guard on either side, and carrying the baskets of berries, approached the flat rock on which sat the immense form of Redeye.

Ju'dal the Human sat beside him, dwarfed by his size.

Neither paid the slightest attention as the two Stoopettes drew near, and it was obvious that Redeye and Ju'dal were struggling to communicate.

The problem was that neither spoke the other's tongue, and the more Ju'dal tried to make Redeye understand him, the more agitated Redeye became.

Lin motioned to Kora to listen in as much as she could, and they took their time in distributing the berries and herbs onto the two plates. Ju'dal had a map laid out between himself and Redeye, and was anxiously pointing out areas of it, gabbling nervously as he did so and keeping a wary eye on the Gork's rising temper.

"Glowurld . . ." he stuttered, ". . . here . . . Source of Light . . ." and he drew a finger out from the Source repeatedly, to indicate rays.

Redeye growled, did the same, impatiently, with his claws; this he understood, but it was plain that that was all he understood. He slapped a huge paw on the map and snarled ferociously, causing Ju'dal to jump.

"How do I extinguish it, Human?"

Kora recognized the words and she almost dropped her basket in shock.

Ju'dal was sweating profusely and were it not for the enormity of his deception, Kora could have felt sorry for him. It would be difficult to feel pity for someone treacherous enough to try to sell the secret of the Light, particularly considering that, in doing so, he was condemning not only his own people, but every creature in the Terrawurld (save the Gork) to certain death.

What could he hope to gain from it himself?

Lin had filled the plate, had lingered over arranging the berries on it, and now she carried it round to where she could see the map more clearly over Ju'dal's shoulder.

"The path to the Source . . . is . . . is . . . thus . . ." quivered Ju'dal. "From here, across to . . . to the Mountains of Separation . . ."

Redeye reached out and knocked the stick from the Human's hand, a stream of guttural language pouring from his gaping mouth which made even the guards nervous, and which Kora recognized as being curses and threats upon Ju'dal for not being able to transmit the necessary information.

Redeye was nearing the end of his patience,

and Ju'dal swallowed hard, his little eyes darting with fear.

Lin, meanwhile, had seen her opportunity, and leaned further over than she should have, taking in as many details of the map as she could in the short time she had.

Kora gasped at her recklessness, and pushed the plate towards Redeye in an attempt to distract him.

But it was too late.

Redeye stared for an incredulous second at the Stoopette who was supposed to be serving food, but who was quite obviously reading the map that the fool Human had before him.

"That one! Kill her!" he screamed in anger, and two guards raced to be the first to do his bidding.

Kora watched as though in a trance as Lin was grabbed and thrown to the ground. In a trice, two four-bladed spears were raised above her; either one would snuff out her life.

"No!" cried Kora, and every Gork within earshot, including Redeye, turned, surprise etched on their faces to hear their own language spoken by a Stoop!

"Kill her, and you'll *never* know what the Human has to say!"

In the silence which followed, she spoke again, the sounds stumbling uncomfortably from a mouth that was not designed to speak them: "I can speak the Human's words to you." She pointed. "But she must live!"

At a signal from Redeye, the guards returned to their stations, and Kora found herself being scrutinized by the giant.

With surprising speed, he shot out a paw and dragged her to him. Twisting her arm so that she was forced to kneel, he cupped one great curling claw under her chin.

"So . . . you speak our tongue," he hissed ominously.

Pik had split his forces, ten on one side of the gorge, and ten on the other.

It was not an ideal ambush point, but the best they were likely to find. The sides of the gorge were not steep, but sloped gently upwards to where Pik and his men now stood, with stout branches which they would use as levers on the dozens of huge rocks which littered the ground.

The plan was a flimsy one, and full of flaws. Only the most rounded of the rocks would roll down the incline and the Gork would probably be able to see them coming and avoid them but, with careful timing, it could prove an effective delaying tactic and might cause some casualties amongst the enemy.

Above all, it would be a message to the Gork

that any element of surprise they might have planned was now destroyed.

As they watched, they saw the first few ranks of Gork line up ready to move on, their scaly skins reflecting what Light there was, a heat haze rising up from their bodies.

Pik checked that his troops were in position, each two behind a chosen rock, knowing which rocks they were to roll next, aiming to have a steady stream of missiles descending upon the enemy. He looked across to the opposite hill, to where Dork-el, son of Dork stood with his ten Stoop.

All was ready.

Lin spread her feet wide, pulling the strangle-vine across her ankles tight as Kora sawed at it with a blunt piece of stone. Any moment now, the guard would return to where he had teth-ered them to a tree, following their encounter with Redeye and Ju'dal.

The full enormity of Redeye's plan was now clear, and the implications of it gave them the energy they needed to try to escape. At all costs, they had to get back to the Sheerstone and warn Klan.

"So, Ju'dal thinks that Redeye is a creature of his word, does he?" scoffed Lin. "That Redeye will let him live in a Kingdom of his own in the Uplands, beneath artificial Light? He thinks Redeye will stick to this promise? Hah!"

Kora continued to saw away. "I care not," she panted. "I care more that it was I who helped Redeye understand what Ju'dal had to say!"

"You had no choice, Kora, blame not yourself. All that matters now is that we carry the warning to Klan!"

And as she spoke, the vine parted.

Feverishly, she grabbed the stone and began to saw at the bindings around Kora's ankles. Several times she had to stop as Gork stumbled by, each too busy with preparation for the march to pay them much attention, and they began to hope that the guard in charge of them had forgotten his duties. The sweat dripped from her brow as the fibres parted one by one. All around them was the sound of hurried movement as more and more columns of Gork became mobile, and each fresh crash of a body through the undergrowth threatened to be the one which would mean their discovery.

The parting of the last strand of vine coincided with the return of their guard, irritated at having been given this extra duty at a time when he should have been advancing with the rest.

Hurriedly, they hid the loose vine ends, and made ready to leap up and run as soon as he discovered that they were no longer tied.

The Gork stomped closer, scowling.

Suddenly, there was a commotion up ahead. Cries of anger and surprise rippled back down the ranks. Gork began running, trampling young trees to the ground in the scramble to see what was happening, where the danger was coming from. The guard instantly forgot them and raced off wildly, his huge haunches shuddering with every stride.

The two Stoopettes could hardly have hoped for such a diversion, but thankful for it, they rose and ran. Bent low, at a tangent to the steady stream of bodies, and making as much use as they could of any cover, rock or tree, they concentrated on putting distance between them and their captors, anxious to deliver their news to the Stoop Council.

A hundred or so leaps from where they began, Kora stumbled and fell over something soft and wet.

Looking back, she and Lin saw that it was the still-warm but headless body of the Human, Ju'dal.

CHAPTER 11

Pik had purposely waited until maybe fifty Gork had walked into the gorge before signalling that the rocks should begin to tumble.

None of the enemy had noticed the onset of the skirmish until the first of the great, jagged rocks was amongst them. Now half a dozen were writhing in agony, and the rest were finding it difficult to turn and escape, so bulky were they, and so densely packed.

Panic followed as rocks rained down on both sides, hitting and setting off others which were lodged half way down the slopes, and the screams of the dying mingled with the cries of anger as those furthest from the carnage realized what was happening, and began to battle through the pandemonium in an attempt to get at the Stoop on the hill tops.

Pik so directed his warriors that they divided their time evenly between rolling the rocks and slinging their reserves of deadly throwstiks into the crowd of reeling bodies. Only gradually did the Gork come to terms with what was happening, and by then, thanks to Pik's strategy and timing, not to mention the accuracy of their aim, the ambush had proved much more successful than the Stoop had dared to hope, and dozens of Gork lay dead or dying.

The Gork fight by instinct and kill by instinct, they know no other way to live, and it is to their disadvantage that they have no system of leadership, no commanders, no marshals, no one (but Redeye) to direct them.

So it was that, as each realized where the threat was coming from, each attacked not as a whole fighting unit, but as the rabble of savage individuals that they were, and they began to swarm like ants up the slopes, roaring and snarling.

The Stoop ceased rolling the rocks, grouped, and loosed volley after volley of throwstiks into the approaching horde. Pik knew that once their ammunition was gone, he and his warriors could last only a short time in hand to hand combat against such superior numbers. His choices were clear – stand and die, or retreat.

His warriors watched for a signal.

The first of the Gork was now only fifty leaps away, their breath could be heard rasping coarsely through their vicious teeth, as Pik drew his hardwood Ka'thuk and held it aloft – the signal to his warriors that the fight was to be to the death.

Suddenly, all over the slopes, Gork began to stop in their tracks. Some began pointing, looking upwards over the heads of the Stoops. Cries of anger turned into grunts of amazement and alarm, then gradually, a silence fell over the whole area. It was as though everyone had been turned to stone: the Gork, frozen, looking up, mouths open, the Stoop, bewildered, wondering why.

So quiet had it become that the groans of the wounded could be heard quite clearly in the gorge below.

"Pik!"

Dork-el, atop the opposite hill, was pointing with his sword. Pik and the others turned.

High above them, floating in the air, was a figure, a Stoop.

As they struggled with themselves to believe the unbelievable, the figure began to draw nearer, drifting ever downward, towards them.

Even at this distance it was clear that the floating figure was that of a big and powerful creature, a fact which made his bizarre appearance all the more intimidating.

All eyes, Gork and Stoop, were on him as he drifted, feet apart, arms stretched sideways, lower and lower.

A murmur of fear ran around the Gork; a number of them dropped their weapons and didn't even notice that they'd done so. The fear spread quickly, sparking off confusion, as their tiny minds tried, and failed, to cope with the inexplicable.

As the flying Stoop came nearer, so they began to back away, slowly at first, then in haste, fearful of being the last to leave, until, in a very short space of time, the whole horde were running like a frightened flock of Ga'zoks, back down the slopes and into the trees.

The figure in the sky was close enough now to show that it was encased in a bubble, the Light from the nearby Glowurld reflecting, rainbow-like, on the sheen on its surface, the occupant's hands pressed firmly against its inside skin for stability.

In awe, the Stoopwarriors awaited its arrival, for by now, being directly overhead, it was descending vertically. Pik thought that there was something familiar about the Stoop, something, perhaps, about the way he held his head, that mane of blond hair, so like Klan the Golden.

They gathered in a circle as the bubble dropped the last two lengths, coming down slowly . . . slowly.

Pik let his eyes wander up the body as it passed him, until, with a jolt, the bubble landed and immediately vanished.

It took a moment or two for Pik's mind to register just who he was looking at, and when it did, the shock of it made him stagger.

"Brog!"

The two friends raced into each other's arms and embraced.

Lin and Kora's attempt at escape had been going well – too well for their luck to last. They had made fair progress whilst their captors had been preoccupied with whatever the turmoil up ahead was, when suddenly they found themselves caught in a wild stampede of fleeing bodies all running towards them.

All around, the Gork were racing in panic, oblivious of whatever was in their path, wild-eyed and frightened. Trapped in the midst of this mêlée, the friends could do nothing but dive and dodge, using their natural agility to outmanoeuvre the bulky bodies coming at them.

More than once they escaped, by a fraction, being crushed to a pulp beneath the massive, charging feet.

In the gaps between, Lin saw a large rock over to their right, and signalled to Kora that they should make for it, and hide there in the shelter of it until the stampede was over. Gradually, they inched their way across, dodging all the time, wondering what it was that had caused such fear in such fearsome beasts. Little by little, the rock loomed nearer until, seeing a space, Kora grabbed Lin by the arm and ran, throwing herself and dragging Lin into the safety of its sheltered side.

Almost at once, they felt themselves falling, realizing too late that the rock had been perched on the edge of a bluff whose walls fell sheer for a good sixty lengths.

Already, the floor of the small canyon into which they were hurtling was littered with the bodies of Gork who, in their flight, had not known it was there.

Jagged rocks rushed up to meet them as Lin, her arms flailing, caught onto a looped tree root which was protruding from the rockface. Her own arm looped into it, and the force of her arrest slammed her head against the wall. Dizzily, she hung there, her right arm a useless limp object, broken.

As her head cleared, she looked down to discover that Kora had not been so fortunate. Her friend lay limp and unconscious – dead for all she knew – across the back of a semi-concious Gork who lay twitching thirty lengths below.

She was too far out from the rockface to be able to get a toehold, and so the whole weight of her body hung on the arm she had hooked around the root. The ache was beginning to grow by the second, and the only thing which kept her holding on was the thought that, if she died, then the information that she had to get to Klan would die with her.

Brog was anxious that his journey to the Source of Light should begin as soon as possible, and Pik was no less anxious to accompany him, but was trying to persuade him to hold back until the arrival of Klan from the Sheerstone.

"Your father deserves to be able to give you his blessing before you go, Brog."

"You are right, my friend. Forgive my impatience, it seems an age since the Light began to fade; I want only to seek a way to return it, and the journey is a long one . . ."

He stopped suddenly, alarmed, his crest rising, then puzzled, held a hand to his brow.

Pik went to him. "What is it, Brog?"

"Planimal!" and Brog saw the look of bewilderment in Pik's eyes.

Pictures were flashing across Brog's mind, a jumble of images, none of which seemed to make sense, but all, he knew, coming to him from Planimal. His eyes glazed, he was turning, slowly, facing different directions, holding his brow in an effort to concentrate, aware that all this would make no sense at all to Pik or anyone else watching.

Pik, indeed, was convinced that his friend was in need of help, but Brog held him off with a hand, his head lifted now, his vision clearing, a purpose beginning to burn in his eyes. He blinked, as though awakening, turned to Pik.

"Four Stoop," he said, "and yourself, come, we must hurry!"

Pik beckoned to four of his warriors, and set off in pursuit of Brog who was already disappearing into the Treelands.

The pain in Lin's arm as she hung from the tree had spread to the whole of her body. Her arm itself was just numb. Time and again she had had to talk to herself to prevent unconsciousness enveloping her, telling herself that she must hang on, must not allow herself to fall to the rocks below, though the nagging doubt in the back of her mind told her that sooner or later that was exactly what had to happen.

The one thought that kept hope alive was that whatever, or whoever, had chased the Gork would happen by and spot her. Her thoughts, too, were with Kora, who had not moved since the fall.

After all these years of captivity – to die like this? But no! She was *not* going to die! She couldn't afford to let that thought enter her head. She *had* to live! *Had* to pass on her information!

Thoughts of Brog came to her, and, had she but known it, it was these very thoughts which the searching mind of Planimal had seized upon and relayed to Brog.

A dribble of grit on her head made her look up.

A face was looking at her over the canyon's rim.

Was she imagining it? Was her pain-crazed mind playing tricks?

The face spoke.

"Hold on, we are with you!"

Something familiar about the voice! Or was there? Had she even heard it?

A stranglevine snaked out by her side, and more grit fell on her as a powerful figure eased its way over the edge and began to climb down.

She saw the blond hair flowing as through a haze.

"Oh, powers that be, let me not fall now!"

Her head began to spin, darkness began to impinge on her vision and she felt the root begin to slip from her grasp. She fell into a dream, and in her dream, she was laughing and running with Brog, her lost love. She felt his strong arm around her waist, and two familiar eyes looked into hers.

A voice whispered, in tones of incredulity, "Lin . . . Lin!"

Then blackness.

CHAPTER 12

Almost two-thirds of the Stoop army, some two thousand warriors in full battlewood, the force which Klan the Stooplord had brought from the Sheerstone in response to Pik's messenger, lay camped along the fringe of the Glowurld as the last rays of the Light slid from the sky.

With the Gork in the vicinity, no one could afford to be caught in a makeshift hollow, and so, with their backs to the flat, barren Glowurld, they faced the fringe trees of the Great Gloom, and rested whilst guards patrolled.

Around a fire against the chill of the coming Blacktime, Brog paced anxiously, casting an eye often to where Lin and Kora lay unconscious, both wrapped in Magna leaves and with healing moss upon their wounds.

Pik watched his friend as he agonized, knowing how he must be feeling having found Lin after all these years, and now, without knowing if she would live or die from her injuries, having to leave on a mission into the unknown – and with no guarantee of his safe return.

Brog paused in his stride as the tall figure of his father paced towards him. Young though he was, Brog's physique almost matched that of the mighty Stooplord, and Klan's expression bore witness to the pride he felt at the way Brog had come through his Growtime.

"You will see that she is tended while I am away?" he asked his father, knowing as he did so that both Lin and Kora would receive the finest attention.

Klan hesitated before answering, his voice too bright when he did so.

"You will be able to tend her yourself, my son."

Brog frowned his puzzlement. "What do you mean? My journey must begin with first Light."

Klan looked uncomfortable.

"Brog, the Council have discussed . . ."

"What is there that needs discussion, Father?" Brog broke in suspiciously.

Klan laid a hand on his son's muscular shoulder.

"Your quest to find the Drabkeeper has been a success that our people will talk of for many generations. Without your information we would be a people without hope."

"What are you saying to me?"

"Now that we know where the trouble is, and that it may be remedied, the Council request that you stand back . . ."

He got no further.

"Stand back?" Brog exploded. "It is *my* quest! It is *I* who must make the journey!"

Pik stepped forward, a measure of his courage to intervene in a disagreement between the Stooplord and his son.

"Brog has my support in what he says," said Pik. "He has worked for the right to carry through his task."

Klan nodded acknowledgement of Pik's support.

"The Drabkeeper thought me fit," continued Brog, "why not so the Council?"

"Brog," cut in Klan, soothingly, "we can send teams of our finest craftsmen, troops to fight the dangers . . ."

Brog turned away, anger simmering, and stared out over the Glowurld where the last flicker of Light sparked on the horizon.

"Teams and troops are not what is needed, Father!"

Now it was Klan's turn to look puzzled.

"How so?"

In his anger, Brog clasped and unclasped the hilt of his sword, the magnificent weapon given to him that very day by Klan himself in token of his achievements.

"Something the Drabkeeper said. He said that the Sickness of the Light could be cured by one brave heart."

He spoke quietly, calmly, and in earnest.

"I have that heart, Father. I want to go."

Klan stepped up behind him.

"Brog, you know the law of the Stoop, the Council's decisions . . ."

Brog spun on his heel, faced Klan with an expression as dark as thunder.

"It was only *I* believed in the Drabkeeper! You thought me fit to search for him even as a Stoopling. Why then am I not fit to travel to the Source of Light and to cure the sickness? Why, Father?"

Klan sighed and continued as though Brog had not spoken.

"The Council's decisions cannot be changed."

"Except by you. You can overrule them. I ask myself why you do not."

Klan's expression did not betray his feelings.

The Blacktime was with them now. The firelight flickered on his noble features as he met his son's eyes and held his gaze.

"Perhaps it is because I know you too well." He paused. "Or have known you too little."

Turning, Klan strode away along the string of fires now burning the length of the encampment.

Brog watched him go, then went over to Lin and sat beside her, her hand in his, and the disappointment burned in his heart.

How long he sat there, staring into the embers of the fire, no one knows, but he became aware of a figure close by him and, looking up, saw that Pik had come over. He squatted by Brog, and there they sat, two brave young Stoopwarriors, friends almost since Birthtime, and sharing now the frustration and anger of being prevented from doing what they believed to be right.

Eventually Brog spoke. If there was one person he had always been able to talk to freely, it was Pik, and he poured his feelings out to him.

What hurt him most was that his own father did not seem to believe in him enough to trust him with the task that he felt he had earned the right to carry through.

Pik was able to put the matter in another light.

"If you had a son," he said, "one who you knew had no fear for his own life, who would risk anything to win through, even if it meant death, and if you had a choice to either send your son on a mission from which he might never return, or to send a team of people instead, which would you choose?"

Pik's words softened the hurt Brog felt, but did nothing to soften his resolve.

"The quest is mine, Pik," he said, calmly. "It has been since the day I ran from the Flatplace. Had I not run that day, in childish fear, my mother would not have had to sacrifice herself for me. This is the way for me to make up for her death, to be sure she did not die in vain."

At the beginning of the next Dayspan, the Carers who were redressing the wounds of Lin and Kora woke Pik as they moved about their business. The wisps of smoke from the dead fires filtered the glow spreading drearily across the flat stone of the Glowurld.

Pik looked across to where Brog lay and saw an empty space.

Dork, Goth, and the other members of the Council were not happy. The team which they had assembled to trek across the Glowurld should have been on its way two hours ago, and would have been had not the Stooplord ordered them to delay.

Now, Klan was telling them he wanted the group to disband.

"How then, do we remedy our position, my Lord?" demanded Dork.

Klan did not reply immediately. He was thinking of the visit he had had from Pik at first Light.

Brog, he now knew, had already begun his quest.

Dork's resounding voice broke in on his thoughts.

"To delay the journey is unnecessary, surely?"

Brog's words kept coming back to Klan as he faced the bewildered Council: "just one brave heart . . ."

Dork spoke again. "The Council demands that the team be despatched within the hour, with Klan's permission."

His son did have a brave heart, he deserved his chance, had earned it, and by now, Klan had made up his mind to give it to him. He dragged his concentration back to the Council meeting.

"The Council agreed . . ." began Dork.

"And I disagree," cut in Klan, and heads turned in surprise. "I overrule."

Murmurs of concern.

"On what grounds, my Lord Klan?"

"On the grounds that my son Brog, without whom we would still be in ignorance, without whose belief and forevision we would still be licking our wounds from the Flatplace, is even now travelling the Glowurld to the Source. It is thanks to him that we have the advantage over the Gork of knowing of the sickness. I believe, as he does, that he can cure it. Above all, I believe that he has earned the right to try."

The Council was silent.

"The Lord Klan has the right to overrule," said Dork eventually. "We ask for a limit to the time given to Brog."

"Seven Dayspans," said Klan. "If, by then, he has not returned, send your team, for by then he will not be returning."

Pik had taken to caring for Kora. Her prettiness attracted him in a way which made him want to see to her needs, to look after her. Now, as he bathed her head, he was distracted by a movement from Lin, nearby.

He went to her as she opened her eyes.

"Pik!" she murmured, a half smile coming to her lips.

Pik sponged her brow. "You are safe, Lin," he assured her.

"I dreamed of Brog, that he and I were playing

together as we used to in our Stoopling days," she paused, in pain. "I dreamed he was here."

"No dream, Lin," smiled Pik. "Brog it was who saved you."

Lin's eyes opened wide. "Where is he?"

Pik told her, and Lin's face took on a great concern.

"Have no fear," said Pik. "Brog can cure the Light, I know it. We can hold the Gork from the Sheerstone until the Light is returned."

"You do not understand, Pik!" Lin gasped, so anxious now that Pik grew alarmed for her well-being. "Redeye! He knows!"

"Knows what?"

"Of the sickness of the Light! He knows, and what is worse, he travels to the Source! Two Day-spans since, he left, with twenty-five fighters! Pik! He intends to extinguish the Light!"

CHAPTER 13

On the hologrammatic model floating before him, the Drabkeeper watched the figure of Brog as he made his solitary way across the Glowurld.

As he watched, he wrote, recording the events as he had done for over three thousand Lightyears.

This was to be the final entry with regard to Brog, for the time being, at least, for Brog was already in the domain of the Glokeeper, and all things Glo were recorded by him.

The Drabkeeper cast a concerned eye ahead of Brog, to where the party of Gork, carrying Redeye, plodded in a straight line towards the

Source of Light, and noted that, across their predicted path, not much further on, lay the one building of any great significance in the whole of the Glowurld – the Glokeeper's castle.

"Oh dear, oh dear, oh dear," he said to himself, and shook his head. "Oh . . . dear."

And, not for the first time in his reign as Drabkeeper, he fretted that the laws of the Terrawurld prevented him from involving himself in creature matters.

All he could do was sit, and watch, and hope, and write in his Record Book.

Biting his bottom lip, and shaking his head slowly from side to side, he wrote a final line, and it said: WHAT MUST BE, MUST BE.

He heaved a sigh, closed his book, laid it aside, and crossed his fingers for luck.

Although Brog's legs were covering the ground at a regular pace, his mind was elsewhere. It was almost as though he was a passenger being carried along, able to let his legs do the work, and his mind do the thinking.

Important though his quest was, he recognized the need to conserve his energies, and from the outset had settled into a comfortable lope which he knew he could keep up indefinitely. He had set out before the Lightime had begun, in total darkness, knowing that, as far as the eye could see, there was nothing to impede his progress on the broad, flat landscape, and he had been running in darkness since, with nothing but his unerring sense of direction to guide him.

The whole of his life had been spent amongst the trees of the Great Gloom. Never before had he felt the experience of travelling a great distance, at some speed, surrounded by nothing, with no twists and turns to make, no rocks or foliage to dodge around, and as he listened to the steady slap, slap, of his feet on the ground, he found the sense of freedom exhilarating.

As the Light had crept its painful way over the hard surface, the reflection from the ground began to make his eyes ache and he thought of wearing the eyeshield that the Drabkeeper had given him, but he persevered, and gradually the ache went.

One thing did puzzle him. The Humans, he knew, lived here, but there were no signs of any dwellings, nor rocks or trees in which they might dwell; perhaps as he neared the Mountains of Separation there would be some evidence of them. He would have to wait and see, for the mountains were still a long way off.

His thoughts, once more, went to Lin.

His love for her had not grown less all the

years she had been away. Her beauty had increased, and there had been a moment, back at the encampment, when he had thought of staying with her, of "standing back" as the Council had put it, but he knew that to have done so would have been to regret it for the rest of his life.

He thought of Redeye and his murdering Gork.

What atrocities would he be planning back there in the Great Gloom?

If Brog could cure the sickness of the Light (and the Drabkeeper had led him to believe that was possible) then the NewBreed would have to retreat to the Darkness. Although this might be seen as a victory, Brog knew that the Stoop would have to find a way to vanquish their enemy completely and permanently, for what they had done once, the Gork might do again, only next time more thoroughly, and a breed of Gork with even stronger eyesight was a possibility which made Brog shudder.

He silently thanked the Powers that he had this advantage over the Gork, this knowledge of the Source. With a little luck, he could turn the tide of battle in favour of his people.

He was so deep in thought that he almost missed the growplot.

Only a waving stem caught the extremes of

his vision, and he stopped and turned back a dozen strides.

A small, saucer-shaped hollow had been dug from the rock, and within it, in soil as black and as rich as any he had seen, grew row upon row of vegetables.

The plot was obviously well cared for, although there wasn't a sign of anyone about. The vegetables were quite well formed but somewhat wilted and undernourished, with any leaves turning pitifully towards the Source as though trying but failing, to eke enough of the weak glow by which to live.

Brog nourished himself, being careful not to take too much of each type of produce, aware that the plot belonged to someone who probably relied upon it to live. He took a last look around, but saw no one. The only visible sign that the plot had been recently visited was a single, five-toed footprint in the soil.

Planimal would have liked it here, but realistically, he wouldn't have made it this far.

All the rest of that span Brog ran, a solitary figure on that great expanse, and with each stride the Great Gloom and all he held dear slipped further behind him. Looking back, all he could see of his homeland now was an indistinct smudge in the far distance, but ahead the Mountains of Separation were becoming more distinct, and he could for the first time make out features on the slopes.

Only when the Light began to fade in the sky did he slow to a walk and begin to look around for a safe place to spend the coming Blacktime.

It was lucky that he was walking for, had he been running, he would have fallen headlong into the hollow that he came across. This one was much bigger, but again saucer-shaped and cut from the stone, and sitting in its centre was what had once been a dwelling.

The destruction was almost complete, and Brog could tell the damage had taken place only recently.

There was enough loose rubble and stone around to indicate that it had once been quite a large building, and in amongst the wreckage, Brog could make out items of furniture, chairs, a table, but what caught his eye as he descended the slope and walked over, was the body draped over the edge of one of the windows.

It was a Human, and he was quite dead.

Brog found five dead Humans in the wreckage, all still warm, freshly killed. They seemed to have put up a tremendous fight for their lives against some sort of vicious animal, and Brog was disturbed to note that the wounds they bore had a strange familiarity about them.

Where had he seen injuries like these before?

He laid the bodies side by side in a quiet corner of the ruin and covered them gently with rock.

The family had lived and died together and now, Brog thought, deserved to lie together in peace.

It was almost dark when he had finished and he decided to spend the Blacktime where he was, so he chose a wall against which to pile stones that he might crouch behind in comparative safety.

It was while he was piling the stones that he came across an item which caused his heart to leap. He picked it up and stared in disbelief.

The Humans *had* fought bravely, and yes, their wounds *were* familiar, for there, before him was a severed hand, not a Human one, but the scaly, three-clawed hand of a Gork!

CHAPTER 14

Brog left the ruined house of the Humans at first Light, but now there was more urgency in his movements, wariness in his manner.

A quick recce of the area around the ruined house showed that the Gork had approached their target at a tangent to his own approach, which accounted for the fact he had not seen Gork tracks so far on his journey.

It also showed the direction in which they had left the scene, and in the fine dust that lay on the hard stone ground, he saw that their tracks lay in a direct line with the Source of Light.

Brog ran on, steadily and strongly, his eyes

on the tracks and the thin line of green blood from the wounded Gork. The need to restore the Light was not now, incredibly, his most important aim. More important by far now was the need to prevent the Source from falling into the hands of Redeye, for Brog knew, as surely as he knew his own name, that the Gork he was following were not simply a renegade bunch who had happened to venture this far. Somewhere ahead of him, Brog sensed the presence of that most hated of all creatures, and his crest rose with the thought of coming face to face with him, this time with a good sword in his hand.

He calculated that they were no more than a good day's run ahead of him. Not only were they more slow-moving than he was but, from what Pik had told him, they would be carrying Redeye. His thoughts turned to what he might do once he had them in sight. A number of things were possible, and all of them depended upon his superior speed. He could see from the tracks that there were about twenty in the group, maybe more, which made confrontation a non-option. Neither could he afford to let them see him. His main advantage, for the moment, lay in the fact that they were, presumably, as unaware of his presence as he had been of theirs until a few hours ago.

Now he saw why they had marched on the Sheerstone in such numbers. It was obviously a ploy to divert attention from this mission, to tie the Stoop up in a battle of defence whilst Redeye and his band attacked the Source.

Not just to attack it, Brog suddenly realized, but to extinguish it!

Brog increased his stride as the terrible truth struck home.

From time to time he came across a spot where the group had stopped to change Redeye's carriers. He could see the marks of the legs of the platform on which Redeye rested, and the scuff marks in the dust where the exchange had taken place. Brog gave thanks for the idleness of Redeye, and marvelled at a selfishness so great that he would risk the progress of his mission for his own personal comfort.

At each of these spots also was a patch of dried green blood from the Gork who was missing a hand, and it satisfied Brog to see that each patch was less dry then the previous one.

The Mountains of Separation were now dominating the horizon, and Brog had already decided that there was really only one course of action he could take which had a reasonable chance of success.

He was, by now, dividing his time between

scrutinizing the trail he was following and searching the horizon for signs that he might, at last, have the enemy in sight. He had to spot them before they spotted him, and when he did so his intention was to skirt round them in a wide arc and somehow get ahead of them. If he could reach the Source before they did and still have enough time to effect some kind of repair, he might just be able to restore the Light fully and at the same time annihilate the Gork, who would die almost immediately on contact with the full glare.

He pushed to the back of his mind the thought that the glare would certainly kill him also.

His head bobbed eagerly as he saw a shape ahead, and he slowed instinctively.

The shape was stationary, and he came up to it fairly rapidly as he realized it was safe to do so.

It was Redeye's platform, abandoned, tossed aside like a huge piece of litter, and not far from it, Brog saw, was the body of another Human, killed as ruthlessly as those he had found in the house, and by his side, the remains of what had once been a larger, four-legged animal. It had been killed and eaten, and all that remained was the head and hooves.

From where the discarded platform lay, new

tracks began. This time the tracks were broad and continuous, the tracks, had Brog been able to recognize them as such, of wheels.

Even though a wheel-bearing vehicle was unknown to Brog, it was obvious from the spacing of the Gork prints that Redeye was now riding on something which enabled his group to move much, much faster than before, and he felt a twinge of anxiety.

The platform, the Human and the eaten animal were not the only objects lying there in the dust. Ten leaps along the track lay the body of the Gork with one hand, a spikeball embedded in his skull. He had obviously become too much of a hindrance to the rest of the party, and they had dealt with him in the only way they knew.

What interested Brog, made his hopes rise, was that his green blood glistened, had not yet had time to dry.

For a while now, as he had been nearing the foothills of the mountains, the terrain had been getting more hilly, and as Brog topped a rise he halted, uncertain of what had caught his attention.

Behind him, the overturned and abandoned platform was still visible as a speck in the distance, but it was what was happening ahead that now took his attention.

The line of the horizon was broken by a single, finger-like turret, and above it hung a yellowish smudge of smoke. As he looked, he could make out the rest of the building to which the turret belonged, and on the right, what looked like the stub of a second turret that had been snipped off, raggedly, like a broken branch.

The smoke was thinning out now in the still air, as Brog tightened his belt and loped off in that direction.

Well before he got there, he could make out the general shape of the building, finely proportioned, square-built, with a turret at each corner, only two of which were still intact. Figures were running from the scene, Humans, heading off in all directions, some passing Brog in the near distance and reacting immediately on seeing him by veering off sharply, suspicion and fear written on their faces.

The only reason the castle was standing at all was that it had been such a substantial building to begin with; as it was, it looked as though a mighty storm had hit it suddenly and ferociously. Every door, every window had been torn out. Black holes in the stone walls gaped like sockets in a skull, and the smoke now rose in a thin column from the centre of the shattered roof.

When Brog arrived, all was still, not a sound

disturbed the air of dread which hung over the place that he knew had once been the Glo-keeper's castle.

Shouldering his way through the broken doorway, he stood in the great hall, his eyes slowly accustoming themselves to the gloom. Everywhere there were bodies: on the steps of the staircase, across the black and white tiles of the floor, on the balconies. All but two of them were Humans, many with their swords still in their hands, and bearing the terrible wounds which only the Gork can inflict with claw, spiketail and fang.

In a corner, as dead as the people they had slain, lay two Gork, with possibly as many stab wounds between them as all their victims put together.

Brog left the hall down a corridor piled high with bodies which included one more Gork. The fighting had been particularly fierce here, as though the Humans had been keen to protect one doorway in particular.

Brog had difficulty in pushing open what re-mained of that door, so great was the number of bodies piled behind it, and, peering through a gap, he could make out a figure sitting in a chair, a very old Human, his white robe soaked red with blood, and Brog had no doubt that he was looking at the Glokeeper.

His anger welled up inside him as he looked at the old man, slain by creatures who would never know the horror of the wrong they had done, would never know the amount of wisdom and knowledge that had been snuffed out by their savage assassination.

The Glokeeper's greatness and goodness was made evident by the way in which so many had fought and died to protect him – all to no avail.

And then, the old man's hand twitched.

At once, Brog sprang to a side window, squeezed himself through, stepped speedily over to where the Glokeeper sat, mortally wounded but, unbelievably, still alive.

He opened his eyes as Brog approached, and far from showing any fear, actually gave a tired smile as though to a friend. Brog could see there was nothing that could be done for him, death was only a short time away.

He knelt by the Glokeeper's side and supported the old man's tired head, feeling helpless, angry, and very sad.

"I have waited for you," said the Glokeeper, to Brog's astonishment.

"Me?"

The Glokeeper nodded, weakly. "You are the Stoop, Brog." A statement, not a question.

Brog nodded.

"You it is with the brave heart," he went on, "you it is who can save the creatures of the Terrawurld."

"I mean to try," said Brog.

The Glokeeper lifted a trembling hand, and pointed to a drawer in an upturned chest.

Brog reached over and opened it, to see that it contained a draw-string bag, and on a nod, he took it out.

The old man's voice was weaker now. He tried to speak, but could not, finally straining forward to find Brog's ear.

Brog bent close.

"Through your enemy will you find success," he whispered with difficulty. "Through me will you reach your goal."

Brog let the words roll around his mind.

"Gather the dust that was me, cast me before you," breathed the Glokeeper, and with a long, rasping sigh, he closed his eyes and died.

As the breath left his body, the very air became electric, sparks crackled around him, bolts of blue static stuttered across his person, and very slowly, starting at his feet, he began to dissolve into a flutter of shining dust.

With alarming speed, the dissolution travelled along the body, rather like a flame along a piece of paper, finally reaching the crown of his head, until all that remained of him were two neat piles of dust, one on the chair, and one on the floor where his feet and legs had been.

"Gather the dust that was me."

The words rang in Brog's head, and carefully, respectfully, he swept every trace of the sparkling substance into the draw-string bag, pulled the top of it tight, and hung it from his belt.

Brog stood for a while, aware of the enormity of the moment, the passing of the creature who had recorded the events of the Glowurld since time had been.

The Gork would pay for this. Not just Redeye's band, but the whole of the Gork nation, in Brog's eyes, had just forfeited the right to remain alive.

Brog stepped from the castle to find the Light very weak, the Blackhours almost upon him. He felt the need to regenerate, but promised himself only a part of the Blacktime to do so. He had to push on.

The stillness was shattered by a cry, and Brog whirled, his hand drawing the sword from his belt. The blade of his attacker was already whistling towards his head as he lifted his sword to block the stroke which would surely have split him open.

Brog parried and dodged, seeing for the first time his assailant, a Human boy, maybe his own age, a look of fierce anger on his face, sturdy muscles straining above the loin cloth that he wore. Brog went on the defence, having no desire to kill the boy, driven back by the sheer ferocity of the attack. Twice in as many minutes, Brog came close to death as the boy thrust and hacked like a madman, striving for a killing stroke. Their sword hilts clashed, and Brog threw the boy away from him, thankful for the break. They circled each other, Brog watching for the next move, the boy waiting his chance to strike.

"Why do you fight me?" asked Brog, his eyes never leaving the scowling face.

In reply, the boy lunged, but missed.

"I am not the killer of your people," grunted Brog.

The merest flicker of doubt crossed the boy's face, though the point of his sword stayed up.

"I *seek* the killers," went on Brog.

"You lie!" Another lunge.

"No."

Still the boy persisted, flourishing his weapon, jabbing and posturing, and Brog could see the hatred smouldering in his eyes.

"Look around you, Drabcreature," he snarled, "and tell me why I should believe you!"

Brog kept his guard, leapt out of range.

"If I am the killer you say I am," Brog spat, "would I now do this . . ."

And so saying, Brog laid his Ka'thuk on the ground.

The effect on the boy was remarkable. His aggression evaporated like a wisp of smoke. The sword point dropped, he looked Brog up and down, as though seeing him for the first time, still suspicious, and not willing to believe.

"Who are you?"

"I am Brog, son of Klan, Lord of the Stoop."

"Stoop are Drabcreatures . . . Drabcreatures did this . . ."

"The Gork did this . . . killed your people . . . as they have killed mine."

Still the boy glared, then turned his head, cast a glance around, the thought that he might have made a mistake finally coming to him.

"I am Brog the Stoop . . . the Gork are my enemy."

The youth sheathed his sword, stood square on to Brog.

"Wrong, Stoop," he said, "they are enemy of us both."

CHAPTER 15

The Gork had not stopped for rest in the Blacktime, that much was certain judging by the age of the tracks that Brog and Jed, the boy Human, began to see as the Light broke over the Mountains of Separation.

They had agreed to a two-hour rest before pressing on into the Blacktime in pursuit of the Gork, and had set a stick in the ground as a pointer to the direction they should take when they awoke.

Even with Jed's knowledge of the terrain, and carrying the same stick between them to avoid losing contact in the Blackness, they could only travel at a fast walk, but now as the way ahead became clearer, and as the mountains began to take on a silhouette, they began to increase their pace.

During their walk through the Blackhours, Brog and Jed had learned a little more about each other and, as a result, the beginnings of a respect between them was starting to form. Jed, it seemed, had been third assistant to the Glokeeper, a sort of researcher who would go out and investigate matters which needed clarification before the Glokeeper committed them to the record books. It was while he had been out on one of his investigations that the Gork had struck.

Jed had been fond of the Glokeeper, who had taken him in as an orphaned baby and had arranged for his upbringing. All the other assistants to the Glokeeper had been killed in the attack, along with Jed's foster parents and all other people that Jed cared about. In one short battle, he had lost parents, benefactor, colleagues, and friends, and at the same time he had gained a hatred of the Gork which matched that of Brog, along with a determination, like him, not to let the Terrawurld fall beneath the heel of the monsters.

They realized that, between them, they had, at all costs, to save the Light Source from being extinguished, and although neither knew how they might go about this, they were united in their agreement that whoever reached the Source first – they or the Gork – would hold the upper hand.

Jed was a strong and an able youth, yet he did not possess the inbuilt stamina of a Stoop and, being only Human, it was necessary for him to stop periodically to catch his breath. He marvelled at Brog's ability to run, seemingly for ever, without a change in his breathing pattern, and began to feel before long that his stops were holding them back.

All that Brog could do was reassure him of how well he was doing, but casting an eye over the mountains which they were approaching, Brog felt apprehension.

It would be a hard climb – even for him.

"The mountains," said Brog during one of their respites, "there is no way around them?"

"They encircle the Valley of Light," panted Jed, shaking his head. "There is no way around."

Something in his tone, the way he said "around", made Brog push his questioning further.

"But to get to the Mound of Extremes, to the Source, the mountains must be climbed?"

Jed hesitated. "It is the only sure way."

"So, another way exists?" probed Brog.

"None that we can use."

"Explain."

"There are the tunnels."

"Tunnels?" Brog's hopes rose.

"But it is certain death to enter them."

"Do they lead through the mountains to the valley beyond?"

"It is said so, but few have returned to tell, and those who have no longer had their minds."

Brog brushed aside his protestations.

"Where are they, these tunnels?"

"Brog, believe me, there are beasts inside the like of which would make a Gork seem like a trained meercat."

"You have seen them?"

"You have only to hear the noises that come from the entrances to know. On nights when the wind carries the sound, the blood can turn to ice to hear it."

Brog shook his head. "My friend, if Redeye reaches the Source before us, then will our blood turn to ice, and that of all creatures."

"Then let us away," snapped Jed, jumping to his feet from the crouch he was in, and in a moment he was off, pounding the ground at a pace far too fast to be sustained for long, anxious to make up for the time he had spent resting. Brog sighed and sped off after him, catching him easily with his long stride.

"Jed . . . slow," said Brog, "slow . . . and regulate your pace."

Jed took no notice.

"Breathe as you stride," urged Brog, "watch me . . ."

He pulled ahead of Jed, and fell into a regular push-push rhythm.

"Breathe out for two strides, in for two strides," he called over his shoulder, "lift your chest, let your legs do the work."

He set the pace for a while longer before dropping back alongside Jed, and was happy to see the boy running more comfortably, his breathing under control.

Jed nodded his thanks. "We will catch them yet," he hissed through gritted teeth.

Brog was beginning to think they might, though overtaking them without being seen was going to be another matter.

Then disaster struck.

In the foothills of the mountains, most of their running had been uphill, though the occasional dip afforded them some relief. As they rounded the corner of a hump of rock, the ground dipped suddenly, accelerating their speed.

Too late, they saw the wheeled cart which had been Redeye's transport. It had been tipped across their path at such an angle that they could not have seen it in time to avoid it; in addition, they were hurtling towards it at break-neck speed due to the slope they were on.

"Jump!" yelled Brog and, banging both feet on the ground, he leapt into the air, clearing the cart whilst performing a mid-air roll, to land squarely on the other side.

Jed was not so fortunate. He tried to hurdle the cart – and almost made it.

His trailing leg hit the edge, and with a cry of pain he landed flat on his back, the wind knocked out of him.

Brog's first thought was of an ambush, but the silence which followed served to show that the cart had been used merely as an inconvenience to any pursuers.

Jed's fall had done no more damage than to give him a severe winding, but his leg was another matter.

The top edge of the cart had been hacked up to produce vicious splinters of wood, and one of these had penetrated Jed's calf muscle, the point of it jutting out, sharply, from the other side.

Jed's agony was evident, though he gritted his teeth and tried to suppress the cry of pain; even when Brog drew the splinter cleanly from the wound, he made no sound.

The open gash looked worse than it was, and after Brog had stemmed the bleeding, and bound it with a strip of cloth, Jed was anxious to be on the way again.

It was when he tried to put weight on the leg that the real outcome of the accident became apparent.

The muscle had been punctured, and try as he might, any attempt to make it function as normal failed miserably. Jed's run was reduced to a galloping hobble, and Brog felt for him as he tried to maintain his speed, throwing the injured leg out stiffly in order to transfer his weight to it as briefly as possible. By the time they had reached the start of the climb that was to take them over the mountains, it was clear to Brog, if not to Jed, that he was in no fit state to make the attempt.

Jed sat on a boulder, the anger and frustration distorting his features, the sweat from his efforts running in rivulets down his chest.

"The fates are against us, Brog," he grimaced. "It will be a slow climb." He looked up at the peaks towering above them. "Too slow."

"Even without your injury, we would not get there in time . . . look . . ." and Brog pointed.

There, high up, maybe a third of the way up the nearest mountain, like a string of ants, they saw the evil, lumbering shapes of the Gork.

Redeye was in the lead, his massive bulk evident even at this range, the whole group plodding inexorably upward and onward with nothing, it seemed, to hinder their progress.

Neither Brog nor Jed needed to say what was obvious to them both: even if they were to begin the climb fresh and uninjured, the Gork would be over the mountain's rim and descending to the Valley of Light, long before the pair had reached where the Gork were now.

They were staring defeat in the face, and they knew it and, as if to punctuate the moment of despair, almost as if to acknowledge their failure, Redeye turned, looked down and saw them.

They felt his glare like a physical presence, and watched helplessly as he pointed; the others turned, saw them too. Then Redeye threw back his head and laughed, the raw, rasping sound drifting faintly to them across the still distance. In a gesture of part-defiance and part-contempt, Redeye bent, picked up a rock and hurled it in their direction. There was no chance of it reaching them, but the action spoke volumes . . . it was Redeye putting the final nail in their coffin. Jed beat the rock he was sitting on in despair with his fists and glared up at the mocking monsters.

"We have lost, Brog," he whispered, "lost!" and a tear of pure anger ran down his cheek. "And evil has won!"

Brog's face was set in defiance. "When the

Light is extinguished, Jed, *then* we have lost," he said simply.

Jed stared angrily. "The Glokeeper taught us to believe that Good would conquer Evil." He spat, bitterly.

"Then believe it," said Brog, "for unless we do, we are all doomed."

"Then tell me, Brog . . . from the depths of all your belief . . . tell me how we can win through from the position that we now find ourselves in – do we fly over the Mountains of Separation?"

"We take the only choice that is left to us," said Brog, evenly.

"And what choice is that?" retorted Jed, but even as he spoke, he knew.

Brog was already striding away as Jed whispered to himself, "The tunnels . . ."

He swallowed back the fear in his throat, and hobbled as swiftly as he could after Brog.

CHAPTER 16

The smile on the Drabkeeper's face was almost as wide as the crater in which he lived.

With the first Light of the Dayspan had arrived three fresh, beautiful thoughts, and he'd been letting them bounce around inside his skull ever since.

Oh, he knew he shouldn't.

He knew that what he should do was release them into the Wurld for some other creature to enjoy, and he would, of course – just as soon as he had finished with them, it was just that they were such beautiful thoughts, wrapped up in so much love, and best of all, they were a present from his old friend, the Glokeeper, or to be more precise, from the Glokeeper's soul, now resting happily in Eternity.

Finally, with a little sigh, and a "Hey, ho hum," he made his way outside to the platform overlooking the crater, running the thoughts through his mind just one more time, then, with a nod for each, he flung them from his head and watched with satisfaction as the sparkballs they produced when they hit the air whizzed once around the great canyon and disappeared over the crater's rim in a trail of glitterdust.

He took a deep breath of the mountain air, patted his chest with both hands and returned inside. The hologrammatic map of the Glowurld still hung in the air, and the Drabkeeper's countenance became more serious as he settled himself to watch the figures of Brog and Jed as they searched along and around the base of the Mountains of Separation for an entrance to the tunnels.

He scowled as he saw that the Gork, with Redeye in the lead, were making better than good progress on their climb, and folding his arms despairingly, he grumped in frustration.

"Rules, rules, rules!" he said aloud. Then, "Laws, laws, laws! Sometimes I wonder why I'm given any powers at all!"

He watched a few moments longer, then the

helpless look on his face gradually began to be replaced by an expression of pure innocence, rather like a naughty child contemplating a naughty deed, but aware that someone might be watching. Casually, he lifted a hand to his head, one finger extended, and made a pretence of scratching his ear. He looked around him, though whom he might expect to be witness to what he intended to do was unclear, since the room was empty. Slowly, he brought his finger forward until it was pointing at the hologram, and specifically at Brog and Jed.

For a long moment he held it there, the struggle taking place within himself plainly visible in the form of a chewed bottom lip, then the finger quivered and began to bend, finally curling fully, his hand dropping to his knee.

The look of frustration returned.

"Rules! Rules! Rules!" he blustered angrily, and swung his chair the other way, activating as he did so the hologram of the Drabwurld which spread out before him like a three-dimensional tablecloth.

With a wave of his hand, he zoomed in on the Sheerstone, where Lin and Kora, their wounds bandaged, were sitting by the entrance to one of the rockholes.

It was a measure of how desperate the situation was that both Stoopettes, despite their wounds, were weapon-making. Kora, who had use of both arms, was threading thongs to a pile of slings, whilst Lin sat and operated a revolving grindstone with her feet, and with her one good arm, held throwstiks against it, bringing each to a wicked point. To one side lay a pile of Magnawood swords and a whetstone.

A busy day lay ahead of them.

A stream of young Stoopwarriors exited from the rockhole and made their way to various points of the Sheerstone as guards-on-watch. One of them was Pik, and Kora called to him as he passed.

Pik strode over, fine in his new battlewood of Warrior-Marshal, an honour bestowed by Klan for his brave attack on the invading Gork three days previously.

Marshal or not, Pik knew his priorities, and took to honing sword edges with the whetstone as he talked. Sharp swords could mean dead Gork, besides, it was an opportunity to be productive *and* be with Kora, and no one who saw them together could be in any doubt that they were very much in love.

"How went the Council?" she asked.

"Not good for Klan," replied Pik. "Dork, Goth, and Kol press him still to send warriors to the Source of Light."

Lin said nothing, but her face registered

anxiety at the mention of the Source; since Brog had left she had thought of him every second of every Dayspan.

"What says Klan?" asked Kora.

"Klan's wisdom amazes," said Pik. "It is as though he can see into the mind of the Gork. Whilst the others fret about the return of the Light, he thinks ahead, plans to rid the whole Drabwurld of the enemy."

Kora threw a glance at Lin. "He is sure then, that Brog will restore the Light?"

"For Klan it is a certainty, such is his faith in Brog."

"Yet he has only four Dayspans of the seven that Klan has granted."

"Dork has a warrior party ready to go now, if Klan were to say 'yes'."

Lin threw down the throwstik she was working on, and the grindstone slowed to a halt.

"And what would that achieve?" she spat. "Either Redeye or Brog are, by now, almost upon the Source. If Redeye extinguishes the Light we *all* die. If Brog restores the Light we live – but not Brog! Not Brog. . . . !"

The tears sprang to her eyes.

"Out on the Glowurld, no Stoop can live when the Light is full. Brog dies, whatever the outcome, and neither Dork's warriors nor Klan's schemes can change that!"

The Drabkeeper whirled in his chair to face the Glowurld hologram, a determined look on his face.

Brog and Jed could be seen still searching for a tunnel entrance, Jed trying gamely to ignore the wound in his leg. The Drabkeeper hesitated but a second, then pointed his finger at them both and nodded.

"Oops!" he said, in mock surprise, and slapped his own wrist.

CHAPTER 17

rog turned to help Jed over a particularly difficult outcrop of rock.

"There can be no tunnel entrances near here, Brog. If there were, we would have heard the Guardians by now."

"The Guardians?"

"Guardians of the tunnels," explained Jed.

As if to coincide with the mention of the name, there came from behind Brog the most fearsome animal roar.

Brog turned, and saw, with as much surprise as Jed, not ten leaps away, set in the solid rock wall of the mountain, a tunnel entrance. It was from this that the spine-shivering roar had come.

The sound of it was still echoing across the terrain as Brog blinked in disbelief.

"The entrance. . . !" he gasped, bewildered.

Jed rubbed a hand over his eyes.

"It was not there a moment ago, I swear!"

They walked over to it, peered cautiously inside and exchanged apprehensive looks at the low growling they heard from deep within.

"Your Guardians seem to be . . ."

"On guard?" added Jed.

Brog led the way, Jed close behind him.

Three or four leaps into the tunnel they noticed that the floor was giving off a glow of reddish-orange light which seemed to be flickering just under the surface, and the ground felt warm to the soles of their feet.

The walls of the tunnel were scarred and grooved. The grooves were in rows as though made by an implement to carve the tunnel out; they looked rather like the marks left in a raw vegetable when bitten – remarkably, thought Brog, like teeth marks.

The curve of the roof was high enough for Brog, the taller of the two, to walk with only a slight crouch, and the friends moved forward swiftly, if warily, making as much progress as Jed's injury would allow.

From time to time they passed tunnel offshoots into which the flickering floor extended, and from these came ominous scuttling noises, and not once were they tempted to divert from the main tunnel that they were in.

The roars now began in earnest, accompanied by high-pitched screams, almost whistle-like, assailing them with an unnerving regularity every few seconds, some of them so loud that they felt almost like a physical blow to the head.

It was impossible to tell where they were coming from, ahead certainly, and from the side passages too, and Jed swore that they were coming from behind as well, and yet already they had travelled some distance without being physically challenged.

The turns and twists in the tunnel made it impossible to see more than eight or nine strides ahead, and they approached each bend with trepidation, never daring to guess what might be lying in wait for them beyond it.

The further they travelled, the more their confidence rose, despite the battering of noise. The scuttling and scraping from the tunnel off-shoots became more pronounced – now they could be heard even before they got to an opening.

On more than one occasion, Brog was sure he saw movement ahead, as though something had ducked inside a side passage to escape them, or at least, to remain hidden.

His sense of direction told him they were travelling, more or less, in a headlong manner, and despite the curves, there was no feeling of having gone in a circle.

Although the incessant roars dulled their senses and confused them, they were, at least, progressing unhindered, even if doubts about the outcome weighed heavily on them.

Brog cast a glance over his shoulder at his companion.

"You are sure this leads to the Valley of Light, beyond?"

"No," said Jed, simply. "I only heard it does."

Brog rolled his eyes and plodded on.

Jed hobbled after him.

Round the very next bend the tunnel ended abruptly.

A solid stone slab, smooth unlike the walls, ran across the tunnel, effectively making any further progress impossible.

One long, moaning shriek came from behind them – then silence, a silence so complete that they could hear each other's breathing. Each read in the other's eyes the helplessness which enveloped them like a fog. After the shrieks, the screams, and the roars that had followed them for so long, the quiet, far from being a relief, was nerve-tingling. It hung thickly in the air, a threat, a warning, a promise, almost, of untold terrors yet to come, and the two companions felt the cold fingers of fear begin to close around their hearts.

They crouched and rested, sweat beading their faces, the warmth from the tunnel floor doing nothing to alleviate the suffocating feeling of being trapped.

And still the heavy silence went on . . . and on.

Jed began to shuffle uneasily, his hand clasping and unclasping the hilt of his sword.

"Why do they not attack?" he hissed.

Brog laid a hand, reassuringly, on his arm. He seemed to be listening, his ears twitching.

"Calm," he whispered, "a little longer."

Jed took a breath, let it out slowly, taking strength from the way in which Brog seemed to be appraising the situation, head cocked, sniffing the air.

A single sound came from the darkness, a scraping, like a claw on stone, and Brog nodded to himself, expectantly, a restraining hand on Jed's shoulder.

The scraping seemed to spread rapidly, being repeated by others, and swelled a thousandfold to a dreadful, rasping crescendo.

Jed's sword was out, his feet spread, anticipating an attack from the unseen enemy.

Brog reached out and lowered Jed's sword arm.

"The sound will stop!" he yelled into Jed's ear. "When it does, then will we attack!"

"If they do not attack first!" shouted Jed.

"Trust me," replied Brog.

Jed nodded, but did not relax his position. The scraping seemed to be getting nearer, and deep into the tunnel, faint spots of white, which could have been eyes, but which could, just as easily, have been a product of Jed's imagination, seemed to dance.

And still, the wall of noise.

Jed threw Brog a look, and struck his sword against the tunnel wall angrily, anxious to resolve the situation for better or for worse.

By comparison, Brog crouched, relaxed, a display of confidence for Jed's sake.

"Think, Jed . . . why do you think they have not attacked before?" Brog called to him. "Why have they not shown themselves?"

"No riddles, Brog, this is not the time for riddles! Let them come! I care not with what weapons!"

"*Fear* is their weapon!"

"They use it well!" retorted Jed.

Abruptly, as though at a given signal, the scraping stopped, and the blanket of silence closed in, once more, around the echoes.

"Now!" roared Brog, and he leapt from his

crouch and led Jed on a mad charge into the gloom.

It was like trying to catch their own shadows. Figures melted away from them as they ran, shouting at the top of their voices along the flickering floor and into the depths of the tunnel.

No matter how they tried, whoever, or whatever it was that they were chasing always kept enough of a distance from them to be unrecognizable.

The air was filled with yelps, barks, and whoops, mingled with grunts, growls, coughs, and any number of less recognizable sounds of agitation.

On they ran, and as they progressed (or rather, regressed) along the tunnel, more and more Guardians were disappearing off down the side tunnels. Brog realized that before long he and Jed would find themselves back at the tunnel entrance, and still on the wrong side of the Mountains of Separation.

Indeed, the thought came to his mind that that was exactly what the Guardians wanted – to be rid of them.

Brog came to a halt, a little too suddenly for Jed, who ran into him and cursed. As they stopped, so did the noises from the Guardians, but almost instantly, from behind, came the familiar roars and chilling screams, a blanket of hideous noise, intended, or so it seemed to them, to discourage them from turning back, to force them on.

"This way," said Brog, and pointed to a nearby side passage.

The tunnel they now entered was narrower and lower, and the light from the floor was barely visible, making it necessary for them to sheathe their swords, and to grope their way along the walls, hand over hand.

"This is madness," muttered Jed.

Brog was inclined to agree, but said nothing.

The tunnel roof got lower by degrees, until first Brog, then Jed had to crawl on hands and knees, and the narrower it got, the more evident it became that the position they were in was indeed a serious one. From the outset, both Brog and Jed had felt a draught from up ahead, a faint current of air which led them to hope that they were crawling towards some kind of outlet, but the walls and roof had narrowed around them so gradually that they had not realized their predicament.

They no longer had the option of turning around; it would have been impossible to do so. They could do nothing but continue.

The hope that the tunnel might lead them to the Valley of Light was now almost gone, yet neither was willing to give up.

They could crawl painfully forward, sustained by a dwindling spark of hope, even though they were crawling towards a near-certain death by suffocation, but to crawl backwards was to admit defeat. Each backward step they took would be leading them to a Wurld from which the Light was to be extinguished, and that would be a Wurld in which neither of them wanted to live anyway.

Jed felt Brog stop and tense.

"What is it?"

"A space!"

Brog had felt the walls on either side disappear. Feeling above his head, he found the roof was gone also.

They crawled a little further, then suddenly, magically, they were standing side by side as the tunnel opened into a cavern. Relief surged through them as they looked around.

The flickering floor spread out before them like a carpet, and sitting in the centre of the whole area was a strange-looking group, almost like a tableau, of creatures.

Their looks, their appearance, did not tie in with anything which Brog and Jed had experienced during the last two hours.

The central figure, like his companions, was furry, with large ears, and probably no taller than Brog's knee. Arranged around him, in a tight cluster, in a way which suggested a kind of subservience, were half a dozen others, shorter than he but, like their leader, their eyes closed as if in sleep.

The half dozen "attendants" (for that was what they seemed) had one small paw which, even as they slept, was stroked constantly over their bodies as if they were in need of warmth. The other arm had no matching paw, but ended in a cruel-looking, crab-like pincer.

These timid-looking bundles of fur, surely, could not be the fearsome Guardians?

The larger creature suddenly snapped his eyes open and focused upon them. He gave no hint of alarm, just stared, in a sad way, at the strangers.

It was as he spoke that the oddest thing happened. The manner of his speech was unusual enough, a mixture of words and growls, but what amazed was his mouth, which expanded and contracted alarmingly with each word, forming trumpets and funnels, chasms and tubes, and produced a volume far, far beyond anything in keeping with his size.

"Whooooo seeeeeeeek yoooooo heeeeeere?" he bellowed.

The Guardians around him sprang awake, their roars of surprise shaking the walls, echoing from the high roof, equalling anything that

Brog and Jed had heard on their trip through the tunnel. As their Leader spoke again, they subsided but glared anxiously at Brog and Jed through enormous eyes.

"Whyyyyy commmmme yooooo heeeeere?"

Brog stepped forward, causing the attendant Guardians to flinch and gather closer to their Leader, whether for their protection, or to protect him, Brog wasn't sure.

"We seek to restore the Light," he said.

The Leader stared back at them. "Thhhhhe Liiiiighhht?"

"The Light," said Brog, anxious to be understood. He crouched, patted the flickering floor. "The Light . . . the Source."

The Leader lifted a hand, pointed to the floor. "Thhhhe Souuuurrcce? Seeeeek yooooo thhhe Souuuuurrcce?"

"To make it well . . . to repair it."

"Thhhhe Souuuuuurcce issss weeeeeeeak."

"We can make it strong again."

The huddled group became animated, bustled, fidgeted, stroking their own fur rapidly now with their one paw.

Once again their Leader pointed with his claw to the floor.

"Thhhhe Souuuuurrcce issss weeeeeeeak . . . issss coooooool."

The others nestled closer to him. It was

apparent that they were trying to provide him with heat from their bodies, probably, Brog decided, to compensate for the lack of heat from the cavern floor. Then it struck Brog – the floor was obviously connected to the Source and therefore would be weakened accordingly. These creatures were probably suffering, in their own way, as much as anyone else in the Terrawurld from the reduction of Light at the Source; if only he could convince them that they would benefit from helping him and Jed.

"Show me the Source," Brog said. "I will make it as before – take away the cold, make the Source strong."

"Maayyyyyyk the Souuuuuuurrcce strrrrrr-ronnng?" repeated the Leader.

Brog patted the floor again. "Strong . . . show me the Source."

The Leader stared stolidly ahead for a long time. Brog cast a glance at Jed. There was no mistaking the hope that lay in his face.

Eventually, the Leader stirred, looked around at his companions and reached out slowly, touching two of his attendants on the head.

They turned, nodded to him, and detaching themselves from the main group, ran over to a side passage where they stood, waiting.

With a wave of his claw, the Leader indicated to Brog and Jed that they should go to the same point, nodding in a satisfied way as they did so.

"Maayyyyykk thhhhe Souuuuuuurrcce stro-ooooooonng," he boomed.

The two attendant Guardians slipped their paws into Brog and Jed's hands and led them into the passage. They went willingly, a new hope rising in their hearts.

CHAPTER 18

The tunnel was lined with Guardians. Silent save for the odd whoop, bark, or cough, they watched from saucer eyes as the two strode by.

It seemed impossible that these small, innocent-looking animals could be responsible for the horrendous noises that had plagued them since they had entered the tunnels, but it was little wonder that, as Jed had related, the only people to return from the tunnels had lost their minds.

In one way, Brog had been right in guessing that their only weapon was fear, for although, in all probability, the one claw each had could have inflicted some damage, especially in a mass attack, the plain truth was that Brog and Jed had not been attacked, and the conclusion was that the Guardians were peaceful creatures whose function seemed to be to prevent access through the tunnels to the Source by outsiders. This they had done for millions of Moonruns by convincing all who approached the entrances that they were far more fearsome than they really were.

As Brog strode along, Jed limping slightly behind him, a hand on Brog's shoulder for support, the reason for the marks on the tunnel walls became clear; from time to time, those lining their route would turn and casually take a bite from the rockface, their huge, elastic lips curling back to reveal strong teeth. The tunnels had literally been eaten away over the generations by the Guardians and their ancestors. Whether the rich brown rock was a part of their diet or not was a subject for debate, but all of a sudden, Brog and Jed felt their bare legs were very vulnerable.

Their emergence from the tunnels into the Valley of Light was an extraordinary experience, and an unforgettable sight. The Valley, like every hollow Brog had seen on this Glowurld landscape, was saucer-shaped, but immense.

The floor glowed and flickered like the tunnel

floors, confirming Brog's suspicion that there was, indeed, a connection, and was so broad that it would have taken half a Dayspan of running to cross it.

Their eyes were immediately drawn to a huge, flat-topped hill in the centre of the Valley, rather like a small mountain whose top had been snipped off to produce a plateau, and even at this distance the surface of the hill seemed to crawl and heave as though in constant motion.

"The Mound of Extremes," said Brog, pointing.

Atop the plateau stood a gigantic, thick disc, like a wheel on its edge, looming high into the turbulent sky, and so immense that, even at this distance, they had to lean back and look up to take it all in.

The Disc jutted out of the plateau, or at least, one half of it did. The lower half was hidden below the surface, inside the Mound.

As he wondered at its enormity, Brog knew that he was looking at the goal of his quest – this was the Source of Light!

The whole Disc was divided into segments, like the spokes of the wheel that Brog had seen on Redeye's stolen cart; each segment pulsated and glowed a dark orange-red, and the whole thing was rotating very, very slowly.

The age-old mystery of the sequence of Light-hours and Blacktime suddenly became clear to

Brog; the segments now below ground, inside the Mound of Extremes, were, he guessed, black; as the Source rotated, so the black segments would rise to the surface and bring about the Blacktime. Even as he watched, a thin rim of the first of the black segments began to appear.

"So big," breathed Brog, in awe.

"How can we, so small, hope to repair *that*?" echoed Jed.

"First, we must find what is wrong."

From a point alongside the Source, piercing the sky like a lance, was a thin, pencil beam of purest white Light which hurt Brog's eyes to look at it.

"There," he said, pointing to it. "I feel that is part of the reason for its sickness."

Jed agreed, it did look like an escape of Light.

They scanned the area thoroughly, but saw no sign of the Gork; it had obviously been a harder climb than they had bargained for.

And so, with Brog wearing the curved eye-shield given him by the Drabkeeper, the two set off in haste, to cover the ground between them and the Source, sitting there in all its immensity, on the plateau that was the Mound of Extremes.

If the trek across the Valley of Light was one of the easier stages of Brog's journey, it was also certainly one of the most awe-inspiring.

The Valley seemed to have a weather system all of its own, which was contained within the Valley and, presumably, ended at the tips of the encircling mountains. Flat, vaporous cloud, the colour of cold lava, swirled overhead, billowing from time to time into dark, twisted shapes, which would swell, erupt, and re-form in the most alarming manner.

Weaving, swooping, and diving in and out of the cloud layer were a collection of the most weird flying animals (they could not be called birds) that either of them had ever seen. Animals with wings which seemed too small to support them, but did; bodies which looked to be mixtures of every conceivable species: fat bodies with spindly legs; feline heads with antlers; hooves where paws should be; creatures half-fur, half-scales, all looking down curiously at the two land-bound animals trekking across their homeland.

The nearer they got to the slopes of the Mound which supported the Source, the more daunting those slopes appeared to be. If they were to reach the Source, there was no doubt that they were going to have to climb to the plateau, and the prospect of doing that was becoming more and more remote.

Eventually, they were near enough to see just what was happening on that ever-moving surface, and the sight caused them to stop and stare in dismay. Had they come all this way, braved all those interminable dangers, to be confronted with this?

The slopes of the Mound of Extremes were, without a shadow of a doubt, impossible to scale!

From the Valley floor to the plateau's edge, and as far as they could see, all the way round the Mound, was a seething turmoil of movement. Thousands of happenings were taking place at any one moment.

Trees rose up from nothing, blossomed, withered and died within the space of fifty heartbeats; dry, sandy areas turned to lush, green pastures, then to stinking, glutinous swampland; isolated areas were being lashed with downpours of torrential rain from the swirling cloud mass above; elsewhere, a blizzard was raging, only for the snow to melt in a twinkling, then reappear, then melt again. Waterspouts careered across the Mound's surface; heavy frost turned to blue ice, ice to water, back to ice, in an apparently endless cycle. Flowers burst open, to die on the instant, only for others to appear and die ad infinitum, glorious swathes of colour crumbling to grey. Waving grassland turned to dust, back to grass; rivers flowed wildly, yet dried to baked mud long before they reached the Valley floor, evaporated completely, and appeared elsewhere.

If ever a place deserved its name, this was it, and whoever had first called it the Mound of Extremes had chosen the name well.

"There *must* be a way," Brog growled, "there *has* to be a way!"

"Not unless we fly to the top," rejoined Jed, and he limped after Brog as, with sinking hearts, they continued their plod towards the seemingly unscalable hill.

It was a moment of near-despair for both of them.

It was also the moment that Redeye chose to top the crest of the mountain behind them.

Hatred and fury blazed from his tiny red eyes as he saw Brog and Jed over halfway across the Valley floor, yet he allowed himself only a low, vicious growl of anger, not wishing to alert them, knowing that now his strength lay in surprise. The remaining fifteen Gork in his party gathered round him as they completed the climb and, scorning the opportunity to rest, he led the way down, his hate-filled eyes fixed firmly on the unsuspecting and vulnerable backs of his enemy.

CHApTER 19

L in stepped into the Council room within the Sheerstone to find Klan on his own at the head of the table, waiting for her.

She was relieved.

Since her summons to attend had been brought to her she had dreaded that the whole Council might be there. Why the Stooplord wanted to speak to her, she did not know; she could only hope that it had something to do with the knowledge of the Gork she had managed to pick up through the Moonruns spent in captivity, that there might be a chance for her to put that knowledge to use, and to help in the fight against the tyrants.

She was not to be disappointed.

From the moment Klan bade her to sit next to him, she could tell by his manner that her knowledge did, indeed, have a bearing on the plans that he was making.

She had seen Klan before, but only when she had been a Stoopling, prior to her capture. She had never been this close to her Stooplord and the air of quiet authority and his royal bearing made her initially timid. Perhaps it was because she now knew that he was Brog's father that she saw the resemblance, the same strong features and kindly, intelligent eyes, and somehow this relaxed her.

Klan wasted no time in greetings other than to nod his appreciation that she had come, and within a heartbeat of sitting at the table she was aware of just why he had sent for her.

"We plan to recapture the Great Gloom," he rumbled, "and to draw the Gork from the Darkness – NewBreed and Old."

For the moment, at least, he was not telling her why, but it was plain that he wanted her to be a part of it.

"How can I be of help?" Lin was surprised at the evenness of her voice.

"You know where the Nesting Stations are," Klan continued, "as does your friend, Kora. We need you to guide us there."

"To destroy the eggs?"

Klan nodded. "That is one part of the plan."

"Consider, my Lord," said Lin, "that even the weakest and most cowardly Gork will fight to the death for the egg."

Again Klan nodded. Lin went on.

"For each other, the Gork have no love, no loyalty, no feeling. Each would sacrifice the other to live, nor for those who bear them do they have feeling. But for the egg, every Gork will lay down his life."

"This I hoped you would tell me," said Klan.

Lin's first thought was that Klan had not understood what she had told him. Why would he want to face the Gork maddened to a raging insanity by a threat to their egg crop? Was she overlooking some vital fact? Or had Klan's mind been affected?

But instantly, she dismissed the thought. Klan was nobody's fool, whatever his intention, she could be sure there was logic behind it, and the good of his people at heart.

She drew the black, shiny hair from her eyes, and waited for his explanation.

"When the Light returns . . ." he began.

She could not stop herself. "If the Light returns Brog will die," she blurted out, instinctively.

Klan regarded her. "If it does not, we all die," he replied.

He hesitated before continuing.

"When the Light returns, we must be ready. We must, by then, have drawn the Gork from the Darkness, every one of them, into the Great Gloom, where they will perish as soon as the Light becomes strong again."

"But, my Lord, as the Light gets stronger, will not the Gork run to the Darkness to escape it?"

Klan used the table as a drawing board, his finger as a drawing instrument.

"If we draw them to the edge of the Glowurld . . . and if we block their retreat, they will perish."

"And how do we draw them to the edge of the Glowurld?"

"We steal away the one thing we know they will search for."

"The eggs!" Lin smiled at the brilliance of the plan, marvelled at the daring, her face clouding only as she realized that the plan was one enormous gamble.

No one could tell if, or when, the Light might be restored. Klan could only guess at the time it might take for Brog to reach the Source.

If he drew the Gork from the Darkness too early, he would have the problem of holding them there until the Light returned, however long that might be, and the thousands of Gork, united by fury at having their eggs snatched, would be extremely difficult to contain.

If, however, he waited too long, and the Light was restored, the Gork, as Lin had pointed out, would simply retreat to the Darkness, from where they would continue to be the thorn in the side of the Stoop that they had always been.

Neither Klan nor Lin mentioned the third possibility, maybe because neither of them wanted to contemplate such a thing, or maybe because both had such confidence in Brog that the thought was not worth contemplating. But, at the back of Lin's mind (and Klan's too, if she had known it) was a terrible thought. What if – having stolen the eggs, having infuriated and united the Gork against them, having cut off the Gork retreat – the Light never came?

CHAPTER 20

There is one quality shared by all creatures of the Terrawurld save the Gork without which all would be the poorer: friendship. The ability to care about another of their own species, or even someone of a species different from theirs. Real friendships last, and one test of a real friendship is that the one who is your friend is in your thoughts, even though he or she may be many leagues away, or 'abs'lan' as the Stoop say.

So it was that, in the Uplands, Planimal sat on the very same rock on which Brog had sat the day they had met, and looked out over the silver-grey, stone-hard Glowurld, with Brog on his mind.

Ever since they had become abs'lanee, when their respective bubbles had parted in mid-air, Planimal had kept his mind tuned to Brog's feelings, mentally tracking his progress, gauging and guessing his reactions to different events, trying, though not always succeeding, in being with him in a telepathic sense.

It had not been too difficult while Brog had been in the Drabwurld, and Planimal's senses had been able to "meld" fairly easily with Brog's. He had even been able to give Brog the mind-pictures which had led him to save Lin's life, but since Brog had begun his journey into the Glowurld to the Source, the contact had been getting weaker by the hour, and now Planimal was struggling to keep open a mind-link with his friend.

He knew the reason. In the Glowurld there was so little plant life, and Planimal needed other plants to act as beacons, to bounce his thoughts from, almost like a stone that skims the water, touching here and there so that it may travel further.

On the occasion that Brog had stopped by the vegetable growplace, Planimal had received such a strong signal that he could almost see him. Then there was a period of time when no signal at all had come to him, as though Brog was no longer on the surface of the land . . . or dead.

Only in the last hourspan, to Planimal's great relief, had Brog's image returned to his mind, a weak link, but one the little creature was glad of.

Now, however, he wore a worried frown, for his senses were telling him that Brog was nearing the greatest danger in his quest so far.

Imagine the sound of a roaring river, a crashing thunderstorm, a torrent of rain, and a howling wind, and now imagine those sounds multiplied a thousand times. Add to that other, stranger sounds, like the noise of a million flowers forcing their way at speed through the soil, of lakes evaporating so rapidly that the water is sucked into the air, or great trees crashing, rotten, to the ground, and you may have some idea of the noise which battered the ears of Brog and Jed as they stood at the foot of the Mound of Extremes which held the giant Disc, the Source of Light, and gazed in dismay at the slopes they would have to climb to reach their goal.

The Source loomed high into the leaden sky above them, one black segment all but revealed, the Light so dim because of it, that Brog was able to remove his eyeshield and tuck it safely into his belt. The pure, white beam of Light still stabbed the sky, but its glare gave Brog no trouble so long as he didn't look directly into it.

Both were struggling with the despair they felt at being so close to the huge Disc whose malfunction had brought such misery to the people of both their races, so close to being able to attempt, at least, to set things right again and to avert the twin disasters which threatened all the Terrawurld – eternal Darkness and Gork domination.

Had either of them turned at that moment to look behind, their despair would have increased a thousandfold for, unknown to them, Redeye and his band of killers had already covered a third of the distance to the Source across the Valley floor. Redeye, fresher than the rest due to his having been carried as far as the Mountains of Separation, drove his underlings mercilessly, as they raced clumsily but swiftly towards the Mound.

Four times Brog attempted to gain a foothold on the ever-changing surface, and four times he was defeated as the ground beneath his feet, or the rock he gripped, or both, changed to a completely different substance, sand, water, grass, or whatever. Jed made efforts of his own at a point a little further along from Brog, but with similar results.

"There *has* to be a way," panted Brog, desperately. "The Source must be reached!"

Jed rested his sore leg, squinting through the sweat running into his eyes.

"If the Glokeeper was alive," he cried above the noise, "he would know!"

Brog hesitated in his fifth attempt to gain a foothold.

The Glokeeper!

What was it he had said to Brog before he died?

He racked his brain and patted the bag around his waist which contained the Glokeeper's ashes.

Something about, "through me . . . through me . . ."

That was it! "Through your enemy will you find success . . . THROUGH ME WILL YOU REACH YOUR GOAL!"

Brog heard again the final words of the old man: "Gather the dust that was me . . . CAST ME BEFORE YOU!"

Suddenly, the words that had meant so little at the time took on new meaning.

Watched quizzically by Jed, Brog untied the draw-string bag from his belt, opened the neck, reached in and gathered a pinch of the glittering dust, then, with his arm outstretched, he let it flutter down onto the surface of Extremes.

As it touched, an area no wider than a

hands, an and as long as Brog's leg, solidified before their eyes.

Brog tested it with a shove of his foot. It was as hard as any rock, unaffected by the turmoil that was going on around it – the beginnings of a path up to the plateau.

It took only a moment for the realization to sink in before Brog leapt onto the path and, followed closely by Jed, began to sprinkle the dust before him, forming a fresh section of path each time he did so, and little by little, they began to make their way up the heaving, writhing slope.

Planimal was agitated.

He was getting intermittent flashes of contact with Brog's sensibilities, and knew that his friend was in the vicinity of some kind of plant life. What he couldn't understand was the way in which the signal kept fading and returning, fading and returning.

He could feel, clearly, the hostility that surrounded Brog, and he redoubled his efforts to remain in contact.

Redeye brought his troops to a steaming, panting halt in order to get a better, steadier view of what was going on ahead. For some time now, he had been able to make out the squirming, treacherous mass that made up the Mound's surface, and had been wondering how, once he had caught up with the two irritants and ripped them to shreds, he would be able to scale the slopes.

As he watched, the saliva dripping in strings from his jaws, a sneer of evil on his face, it seemed that the problem was being solved for him. With a grunt, he waved his Gork forward, confident now of success, anticipating the joy of blotting out the hated Light forever.

Still unaware of the approaching Gork, Jed and Brog inched their way along the narrow pathway, all their efforts concentrated on keeping their balance, knowing that one slip could send them headlong into the swirling mêlée, and death would follow – and a slow death most likely. More than once, the branches of a rising tree thrust their way across their path, narrowly missing their legs, and the tumbling waters of a rushing river plucked at them like a giant hand, but through it all, the strip of walkway remained firm to their tread, and carried them, step by cautious step, further away from the Valley floor.

Brog was laying out the most direct route to the top, though occasionally he had to divert to avoid odd lumps of rock that protruded, and which were unaffected by the constant surface changes, probably a part of the underlying rock of the Mound over which flowed this river of constant movement. These boulders offered slight relief for their tense muscles, and welcome resting places.

It was while they were clinging to one of these rocks, like stranded Krabs, trying to regulate their breathing and gathering strength for the next stretch, that Jed happened to glance out over the Valley. What he saw almost caused him to lose his balance.

In the nick of time, Brog grabbed the neck of his tunic and pulled him back to where he could grip the rock. In doing so, Brog saw the danger that had so startled Jed.

There, well into the last half of the distance to the foot of the Mound, their blue-black scales reflecting what Light there was, grunting with effort, raced fifteen hated Gork, and stomping ahead of them, his hind legs swaggering, lizard-like, ran the gargantuan figure of Redeye, the two orbs which gave him his name burning brightly in his head, his great mouth gaping wide.

The sight galvanized Brog into action.

Working methodically, and with an urgency worthy of the situation, he put everything into the all-important task of reaching the plateau as quickly as possible. All of a sudden the neck of the bag seemed narrower than it had been, his three fingers became clumsier in his haste, and he had to fight to prevent desperation from creeping into his efforts.

Jed remained close behind him, frustrated at not being able to do more, clasping Brog's belt to give his friend the stability he needed to make progress. Brog set up a rhythm of dig, sprinkle, shuffle forward, dig, sprinkle, shuffle forward, sometimes hardly waiting for the path to solidify before stepping onto it, and all the time, in the back of his mind was the soul-destroying thought that he was also laying the path up which Redeye and his murderous bunch would be able to scramble.

They were now beginning to make more rapid progress, but had to abandon some of their earlier caution to do so. Looking back, they could see that the rock where they had re-doubled their efforts was already far below them. The rim of the plateau was only perhaps fifty leaps above their heads, but the Gork were on the last run-in to the start of the path they had laid.

Brog began to wonder what lay on the plateau. Would it be solid? Or would there be more treacherous surface to cover before they could actually get to the huge Disc, which stood now like some immense circular Colossus directly above them, the two remaining Light sections gleaming like the eyes of a dying giant.

Brog found that, even in the face of the terrible dangers that threatened him, thoughts of Planimal were on his mind, calming him, steadying his nerves, somehow helping him to reason and remain cool, as slowly but surely, the plateau rim drew ever closer.

Below, closing rapidly on the foot of the Mound, Redeye was unable to contain a roar of triumph. The others joined him, and the dreadful sound filled the Valley of Light, driving the flying creatures away and into hiding and drifting up to Brog and Jed, just as Brog reached up and dragged himself above the lip of the plateau.

The single, pencil beam of pure, white Light was too bright for him at such close range, and he had to don his eyeshield before he could take stock of what he saw.

As he had feared, the flat top was a part of the surface of Extremes, except for a huge plinth of rock in the centre which held the Source. The beam of escaping Light shone through a hole in this plinth, and it was obvious to them both that one of their first tasks would be to plug the gap through which it was escaping.

But first, they had to traverse the plateau and reach the plinth itself.

They began to ease their way across, thankful that the climb was completed at least, and as they did so Redeye set foot on the beginning of the path below them.

They were six leaps or so from the plinth which held the Source, when Brog reached into the bag and his fingers encountered . . . nothing. Feverishly he yanked the neck of the bag fully open and peered in, before turning it inside out.

It was empty.

Their hearts sank. A gap of six leaps separated them from their goal, and they had no means of covering the distance. They stood, trapped, unable to advance, even less able to retreat. This, indeed, must be the end.

The only consolation was that it was also the end for the Gork, for neither would they be able to cross the gap. Powerless, how long they stood there they didn't know, an age it seemed, during which each drew his weapon and turned to face the evil which they knew must creep over the rim at any moment.

Following their Leader's example, the Gork used forepaw and hind leg to traverse the narrow path, their tails swinging to keep a balance. Even so, two were swept from their perch by upthrusts of trees, and one blown off by a sudden hurricane of wind, to be swept away by a river and dashed to death on a rock.

Nevertheless, they were able to travel the length of the path much faster than Brog and Jed had done, and neared the plateau rim at an astonishing speed.

Brog, facing the rim, turned at an unusual sound behind him, unusual even amidst this vast cacophany, and found himself blinking in disbelief at what he saw happening. He clasped Jed's shoulder, and he too turned, to see that long-stemmed creepers on either side of the gap were stretching themselves to cover the area.

As they crossed each other's paths, they inter-twined, weaving themselves into a mat of veg-etation which, even as they watched, grew to cover the surface and bridge the space between the end of the path where they stood and the rocky plinth which held the Source of Light.

"Planimal!" whispered Brog, unaware of Jed's puzzled frown as he did so, but certain in his mind that this was, indeed, the work of his abs'lan-ed friend. "Quickly!" and he and Jed ran swiftly across the living carpet to the plinth.

Any joy they might have felt at reaching their goal was denied them by the thought that, at any time, the Gork would appear above the rim, and before that happened, there was so much to do, so much to find out about the nature of the huge Disc, and so very little time to do anything.

Brog and Jed had long since resigned themselves to the fact that they were going to die; they would give their lives willingly if only they could achieve what they had come to do. It was a matter now of how much they could achieve before death finally overtook them – before time ran out. Motioning to Jed, Brog set his shoulder to a loose boulder which lay nearby, and between them they rolled it to the hole through which the beam of Light was escaping.

If only this was the whole fault, this escape of Light, the reason why the Source was not getting enough power, then their problems would be over! They held their breath as the boulder sank into the hollow surrounding the hole, blocking it, cutting off the beam as a knife would slice a vine. Would this have an effect? Would the remaining sections of Light begin to burn brighter? Would the Disc turn faster?

Their hearts sank as they realized there was to be no change at all, that the escaping beam was not the fault they hoped it would be.

Brog removed his eyeshield, and turned in time to see the huge, scaly hand of Redeye claw its way over the rim, to be followed by his evil, terrifying face.

The monster turned his eyes on the pair, fixed them with a glare of pure hatred, and as he hauled himself over the edge and stood erect, dread pierced their hearts.

Redeye knew he had won.

All he had to do was wait until the black sections of the Disc were all above ground, then jam the Disc at the point where it sank below ground level – any of the slabs of stone lying around the plinth would do the job – and total Darkness would be achieved for all eternity.

Little wonder then that he took his time, at this moment, to gloat, to leer, to laugh at these two pathetic creatures, one Stoop, one Human who, even though defeat stared them in the face, still stood side by side, swords in hand, with a look on their faces which was meant, he supposed, to give the impression that they were dangerous.

He threw back his head and laughed, his cancerous yellow fangs showing starkly against the red of his throat.

Idly, he surveyed the last few leaps to the plinth, saw the matted, twisted layer of vines, and his eyes narrowed with suspicion.

Stepping aside onto a rock, he motioned the first of his warriors forward to test its strength.

Brog and Jed tightened the grip on their swords as the Gork edged his way forward along the remaining path and onto the vine matting. It sagged, but held, and as he crept cautiously forward, first one, then another of his companions joined him.

From the corner of his eye, Brog saw the ends of the vines begin to unwind, to disentangle themselves, and come apart. Planimal was at work again! Co-operating with the kindred spirit of the plants, he was enlisting their help.

Too late, the three Gork tried to scramble for the plinth. They never made it.

As the vines retracted and separated they were thrown, screaming into the surface of Extremes, to die horribly, as the force of a hundred different elements exerted themselves.

Brog and Jed smiled grimly to each other, glad of this small consolation, happier now that the gap had opened up between them and the foe. Even though it didn't improve the chances of their ultimate survival, it did give them a breathing space in which they could look around, maybe discover what needed to be done to right whatever was wrong with the Source.

Redeye's rage was boundless, not because he'd lost three warriors, but because his moment of triumph had been snatched from him. He realized the danger of allowing the two time in which to work, and anxiously looked around for a way, any way, to get to them and to the Source.

"While we have time," urged Brog, and sheathing their swords, they turned to the task of inspecting the Source and the plinth of rock on which it stood, in the weak glow which emanated from the one remaining section of Light.

The more Redeye pondered, the angrier he became and his fury was awesome to witness. He raged and screamed, lashing the air with his spiked tail, shaking the scales around his chest until they rattled and clashed even above the noise of the writhing surface.

The others cowered, terrified, as he screeched at them in the ugly, guttural grunt-language of the Gork, driving them, with blows from his huge fists to the end of the pathway and onto the jut of rock which lay there. They cowered, wild-eyed, aware of what their Leader would force them to do.

Spurred on by Redeye's savage rantings, the frightened Gork climbed atop each other's shoulders, winding their tails around each other for support, then half stretched, half fell into a position from which the foremost creature could grasp the end of the plinth, forming a precarious and temporary bridge. No sooner was the connection made, than one other ran across, jumped onto the plinth and held the wrists of the Gork who was struggling to maintain a grip. Seeing that the living bridge was now a little more secure, Redeye stepped onto the backs of his troops.

On the far side of the Disc, Brog and Jed had found something – what appeared to be a stone trapdoor set in the plinth. Jed was in the act of scraping the dirt from the crack around it when they heard shouts and screams. Leaving Jed to continue the work, Brog ran to where the gap had been.

The gap was still there, but so were the dying bodies of the band of Gork, screaming in agony as each died a different death in the turmoil into which they had fallen. As he watched, the bodies were swept away, tumbling and falling, broken and battered, off across the plateau and on down the Mound to be scattered and churned into fragments for ever more.

Brog smashed a fist into his open palm in delight; with the enemy now removed, they could search for the fault in a more thorough manner.

He turned to rejoin Jed to tell him the good news.

Not five paces away, Redeye stood, glaring his hate, a spikeball in his hand, and a look of triumph on his face.

CHAPTER 21

The dampness trickled down the bark of the trees, and a deep root-mist swirled around the close-knit trunks.

Amongst the trees bordering the Glowurld, spread over a distance of maybe a hundred leaps, all but hidden by the swirling mist, exhausted but triumphant, lay Lin and ten hand-picked Stoopwarriors.

Cradled in her one good arm lay a Gork egg.

She looked along to where the six Stoopettes, freed from the Nesting Station only hours before, crouched, each with a carrysling around her shoulders, each carrysling containing two eggs.

By her side, watchful, alert, strong and fresh as he had been when they had begun their mission at first Light, squatted Klan, his keen ears twitching, head bobbing as he peered in all directions, assessing the effect of their actions that day, weighing the position of his group of guerrillas.

The whole of the Great Gloom seemed to be alive with the sound of Gork.

From every direction came the growls and roars of angry creatures, the crash of bodies through the undergrowth, and the frustrated howls that accompanied their frantic search for the stolen eggs.

Klan smiled grimly at the sound, and nodded in satisfaction. It had been a good Dayspan, and he took his mind back over the proceedings.

All had been quiet at the Nesting Station that morning. The two Gork guards had been patrolling sullenly, unaware of the Stoop presence in the bush not ten strides away.

Lin, Klan and the dozen Stoopwarriors had lain hidden, watching closely as the female Stoop prisoners had tended the hateful, pale orbs which were the future generation of Gork. There, on the very borders of the Darkness, the Light had never been adequate even in the days before the Source had been disrupted; now, in the early Light from the dying Source, the hidden Stoop were struggling to maintain their vision, their eyes fully enlarged.

Klan knew that, due to the timing of the mission, the strike would have to be very soon.

Ten leagues away to their left, Kora, Pik and a similar number of Stoopwarriors crouched, waiting to strike Nesting Station Number Two, whilst even further along the fringe of the Darkness, poised for their attack on the third and final egg-clutch, were Dork-el and his party.

The plan had been the same for all of them, and had three main aims: to capture as many eggs as they could carry without hampering their flight or forfeiting their ability to defend themselves; to attract as much attention as possible in doing so; and to escape.

If they had time to destroy the remaining eggs, then that would obviously be a bonus.

Klan had every faith in the leaders of the other parties, Pik and Dork-el. They would adopt the best plan of action to suit their circumstances; he had long since decided how he would deal with his particular situation, and each of his warriors had known exactly what was required of him.

Five warriors would attack the first guard, Klan himself would see to the second, leaving Kora, seven warriors and the six Stoopette prisoners to destroy and capture what they could. The deadly Ka'thuks, oiled until the Magnawood gleamed, sharp and hard as flint, had been out and waiting long before Klan dropped his hand in signal.

Neither guard stood the slightest chance.

The first had slid to the ground with the look of surprise still on his face, his heart lacerated by a flurry of vicious swordthrusts, and before his legs had stopped twitching, his executors had been in amongst the rows of eggs, slicing the hated pods, making the air redolent with the stench of the putrid contents, everywhere the hiss of escaping life-gases.

The second guard was meant not to die so easily.

He had always been their best chance of attracting the attention of the rest of his kind, and all that Klan had needed to do was slash the tendons behind his legs, and those leading to his tail, leaving him incapacitated, and a witness to the destruction of the egg-clutch.

His roars of surprise and pain had been nothing compared to his screams of fury as he lay helpless and watched the eggs being systematically smashed by the Stoop. It had been exactly as Lin had predicted; so great was the instinct of the Gork to protect the egg, that it prevailed over all other instincts. The effect had been clear to see in the immobilized Gork. In normal battle conditions, his injuries would have been enough to prevent him from taking any further part in the fight.

The Gork are not known for their courage, but as he had seen the destruction, he had actually tried to drag himself forward in a futile attempt to stop what was going on.

His cries had alerted other Gork, who had rushed to the spot, not to his aid, for Gork have no sense of helping each other, but to protect the egg crop.

Klan and his party had stayed as long as they had dared, only making a swift exit on Klan's order, taking with them twenty eggs, and the astonished Stoopette prisoners, and leaving behind a Nesting Station which looked as though a mountain had fallen upon it.

The rest of the day had been spent running, hiding, and fighting off any Gork they had come across in their retreat. Two Stoopwarriors had been lost in one such action when a Gork appeared unexpectedly from the trees. The damage had been done before the rest were able to hack him to pieces.

At all costs, the groups which had attacked all three Nesting Stations had had to stay ahead of the Gork, attempting to draw as many as possible well into the Great Gloom, where they would be vulnerable to the Light if and when it was restored.

Crouching now in the mists at the end of the Dayspan, Klan pondered their predicament. Lin had accurately described the Gork concern for the egg, and if the sounds they were now hearing were any indication, there seemed no reason why the whole of the NewBreed could not be drawn into the exposed area. The nearer they were drawn to the edge of the Glowurld the more devastating would be the results when (and if) the Light came flooding back.

It was that 'if' which troubled Lin as she lay there watching the last faint glimmers die.

No one had spoken of what the outcome might be if Brog failed in his quest. Even if he *was* able to restore the Light, would it eventually shine out over a Great Gloom littered only with the bodies of those who had committed themselves too early, who had had to wait too long for their salvation?

CHAPTER 22

Brog leapt aside as Redeye's chained spike-ball swung through the air and bit chunks from the stone plinth where he had been a split second ago.

He ran along the plinth, passing in front of the Disc, and rounded its thick edge to the far side.

Jed was on his knees about halfway along, scraping feverishly in the rock with his sword point, removing the dust of ages from the gap around the trapdoor they had found.

"Jed!" he called as he ran to him, "Jed!"

Jed turned.

"Redeye!" yelled Brog.

Even as he uttered the hated name, the massive frame of the Gork leader, big even in relation to the Disc they were standing by, appeared around the Disc edge on the far side of Jed.

Jed spared him hardly a glance, and continued to scrape with renewed vigour. Looking over Jed's shoulder, Brog saw that the trapdoor had a central stone ring-pull.

Brog's heart leapt.

"Will it open?" he yelled over the surface noises, which seemed to be even louder on this side of the Disc.

Jed shook his head, scratching furiously.

Redeye slowly took stock of what was happening, decided that the time was his, and began to swagger forward, swinging his spike-ball as he came. Jed frantically cast aside his sword, grasped the ring-pull, nodded for Brog to join him, and together they heaved for all they were worth, the veins of exertion standing out on their temples.

The trapdoor remained firmly fixed, and Redeye, leering, paced closer, confident that he had them, enjoying their panic.

Feverishly now, the two drove their sword points into the crack around the door, scraping and scratching furiously, so that dirt and grit positively flew from the gap. Redeye was so close now that they could hear the rasp of his breath, the creak of his scales.

One last try.

Together they sheathed their swords, grasped the ring, bent their knees and leaned into the pull.

Nothing . . . and then . . . yes! A chink of Light!

The trapdoor moved a finger width, not even that.

Brog felt a stab of pain behind his eyes as the Light filtered through, and quickly straightened to put his eyeshield on before bending once more to the task.

Redeye stiffened anxiously as he sensed the new hope they felt, read it in their movements, and he quickened his pace.

"Now, Jed! Our last chance! With all your might!"

The stone square lifted and slid over, and a shaft of brilliance shot skyward.

Taken unawares, Redeye, not two leaps off, staggered back, clutching his eyes, bellowing in pain, and the two friends grasped their opportunity. Brog followed Jed through the hole and into the space beneath the Disc.

The opening was far too small for Redeye to follow, even if he had been able to; as it was, the monster lay, temporarily blinded by the glare, beating his fists into the stone in his anger.

They did not drop far, maybe two lengths, and as they gradually became accustomed to the brightness, saw that they were on a wide ledge. The Disc hung down below the ceiling almost within arm's reach of them, and the curve of it dipped away below their level.

Brog gave silent thanks for his eyeshield. He knew that without it, the intensity of the Light would have exploded his brain. Redeye's eyesight came back to him slowly, and his pounding head subsided as he lay, face down, the part-open trapdoor at his feet. So, he had been denied the pleasure of killing the two insignificants. What matter? They were as good as dead anyway. All he had to do was push closed the trapdoor and they would be sealed away for ever, and once he had jammed the Disc, his mission would be complete. Then he could put his mind to getting off this forsaken Mound and back to his people, whom he would lead in triumph across the Terrawurld.

Washing the indignation of Brog and Jed's escape from his mind, he eased himself backwards, eyes closed tightly, until he felt the square stone trapdoor lid with his feet, and began to manoeuvre it into position over the opening.

Brog and Jed swapped anxious glances as the

lid thudded into place. At first glance there seemed to be no way off the ledge they had dropped onto.

Brog answered the unspoken question in Jed's eyes with a shrug.

Jed looked over the edge into the bright depths of the cavern which housed the lower half of the Disc, before crawling after Brog along the ledge in the only direction possible.

Ten leaps on, Brog stopped, waiting for Jed to catch up, and when he did, it was to find Brog pointing down a winding flight of stone steps, dust-thickened by Moonruns of disuse, and leading, it would seem, to the very floor of this immense cavern.

Without hesitation they began the descent, treading warily on the crumbling steps, which led down in an unbroken spiral. Each turn gave them a better view of the Disc, its great segments of Light pulsating in a half-glow, and Brog could only imagine the intensity that would ensue if all those segments were working on full power.

The steps did indeed lead them to the cavern floor, where eventually they stood. The Disc dipped down from the roof in an awesome curve until it almost touched the floor, still turning ever so slowly, the rim of the final black segment about to disappear into the ceiling high above. Here, the glare was at its most intense, Brog's eyes had begun to ache despite the eye-shield, and Jed had to shield his own eyes with his hand.

The main cause of the brightness was the beam of pure Light which they had blocked off on the surface. It came from a deep crack in the glowing floor, and shot rod-like into the air where it hit the cavern roof right alongside the Disc. Now denied access to the outer world, it cascaded over the roof like a waterspout.

Jed was searching the walls around.

"There seems no way out, Brog," he called from across the floor.

Brog was standing motionless, surveying the Source.

"Brog?" called Jed, and strode over, keeping his face turned from the intensity of the beam. "Did you not hear me? There is no way out! We are trapped!"

Brog nodded slowly, spoke to himself, without looking at Jed.

"I see it now . . ." he murmured.

"What? See what?"

Brog pointed. "The Source of Light. It comes from the ground. It comes from that crack."

Jed shielded his eyes, looked. "And so?"

"It is the driving force of the Disc, and yet . . ."

Jed followed Brog's gaze upward. "It wastes

itself on the roof since we blocked the hole."

"It should . . ." began Brog, then realization came to him. "The ground-shake!" He clapped a hand on Jed's shoulder, causing him to wince as the jolt ran down his injured leg. "The groundshake has diverted the Source! The beam should be falling upon" . . . he studied the Disc, the angle of the beam, the gap it was emanating from . . . "there!"

He pointed up to the centre of the Disc, the hub, a huge, transparent, concave circle just below the roof.

It made sense.

To generate full power, to provide Lightime and Blackhours as normal, the pure beam of Light, the Source beam, would have to be concentrated fully upon the centre of the Disc, to power it. The Disc was now operating, presumably, on the glow being given out by the Source beam, the column of pure Light now splattering itself across the cavern roof.

They had discovered the fault.

Even as the truth of the matter dawned upon them, their hearts gave a lurch as, with a crunch, the Disc came to a shuddering, groaning halt.

Redeye, above, roared in satisfaction as he wedged the slice of rock into the gap between the Disc and the plinth, and the whole Terrawurld was trapped in eternal Blackness.

CHAPTER 23

They had searched every inch of the cavern walls, as high as they could reach, except for the area around the Source beam where neither could stand the intensity, without success.

Brog had even searched the walls up the staircase to no avail, and the ache in his eyes now was so intense that his head was beginning to throb.

Both of them had to keep their backs constantly to the Source beam in an effort to lessen its effect on them; even so, the glare reflected from the walls seemed to creep behind their eyeballs, and no matter how tightly they closed their eyes, the brightness sent whirls and zig-zags of stabbing pain shooting through their temples.

In addition to this, the glow beneath the floor seemed to have increased in intensity since the Disc had stopped turning, and was giving off more heat.

Just how long either of them could stand the bombardment they could only guess.

Slowly, the pressure began to take its toll. They felt weak and sick, and as they crouched as far from the Source beam as possible, it began to feel, for both of them, terminal.

They were to die a long, lingering, painful death, trapped in the bowels of a mountain.

Ironic, thought Brog, that he and Jed should die from too much Light while their people died from a complete lack of it.

It was then that Brog heard a sound, a crunching, and at the same time, grit and dust began to fall on his head. Squinting, he could vaguely make out the wall which he was facing, and imagined he saw movement there.

The rock appeared to be crumbling before his eyes.

Was it another ground-shake?

But no ground-shake had ever been accompanied by such a regular, rhythmic, 'crunch, crunch'.

He shook Jed, and the boy Human raised a weary head, shielding his eyes.

Chunks of the wall were now falling, and even as they watched, an opening appeared, only as big as a fist at first, but rapidly widening as, all around its edge, they saw the teeth and jaws of half a dozen Guardians, biting and chewing and slowly revealing a blessedly dark hole leading to a passage beyond.

No sooner had the hole been made wide enough for the two companions to crawl through, than the unconventional excavations came to an abrupt halt, and the tiny creatures who had eaten their way through stood back and invited them to pass.

As far as they could make out the tunnel was a new one, eaten out with the sole intention of reaching the trapped pair, and although its floor glowed just as brightly as the cavern floor had, by comparison it was cool and dark, and both Brog and Jed could feel their pain receding as they followed their saviours back along the shaft to a point where it joined a small chamber.

The arrival of the Guardians had been the last thing they had expected to happen, but what they saw when they stepped into the chamber was almost as unexpected.

It seemed that their rescuers were amongst the most hospitable creatures in existence.

It was incredible that, only hours before, they had tried so hard to discourage the two from even entering the tunnels, for now, spread temptingly on a great rock slab, was an array of vegetable foods and a quantity of sweet spring water, provided, it would seem, for them alone, for no sooner had they been led into the chamber than they found themselves the sole occupants of it, their guides having melted, as it were, into the tunnel entrances which ringed the chamber.

Certainly, neither of them had realized until then just how long it had been since they had eaten and drunk, and both vowed that, should they live for ever, they would never again taste food or drink quite like it; simple though it was, it was like a banquet to them, nourishing, life-giving, and very, very welcome.

They took stock of their situation. Redeye, having shut down the Disc, was now trapped on the plinth of rock surrounding it, with no way of getting down from the plateau. They could leave him there to rot, of course – a death too good for him, they both agreed – but that could take a long time, and each Dayspan of Darkness weakened the Terrawurld a little more, gave the Gork a firmer foothold.

No one in the Drabwurld or the Glowurld realized that the Blacktime they were now experiencing was the start of a potential eternity of Darkness, that the Lighthours they were expecting were never going to come.

In the quiet of the chamber, weary, and for the moment unthreatened, Brog's thoughts turned to Lin. She had looked so beautiful; would he ever see her again? Was she, like the rest of his people, doomed never again to see the Light? To wander in a Great Gloom dominated by the Gork, waiting her turn to be devoured?

He thought over his days as a Stoopling, how he and Lin and Pik used to run and play through the Light-dappled trees around their hollows, swim in the clear lake by the Flatplace, and chase the wild lopfurs around the hillocks and into their burrows.

He heard again his mother's call and saw her striding through the long grass towards him, a pannier over her arm full of wild fruits; and when the Blacktime drew near, sometimes Lin and Pik would come and share their hollow, the warm, safe, dry hollow which Blid had dug and furnished herself, filled with the smell of pine berries and muskbread.

Brog blinked himself awake and looked around.

The first thing he noticed was that the floor of the chamber was distinctly more bright than it had been when they had entered, an orange, as opposed to the orange-red it had been before, and quite a bit warmer to the touch.

By his side, leaning against the wall, Jed was asleep.

Hearing a scuffle, he looked up and saw that the remnants of the meal that had been laid out for them had gone, and where the table had been now stood a group of Guardians. Brog recognized the taller one in the centre of the group as the Leader he had previously spoken to, when was it? One Dayspan ago? Two? It seemed like a hundred.

There was something different about him, indeed, the whole group had changed in some way.

It was a while before Brog realized it was their skin. Instead of the covering of fur, they now sported a light covering of down through which a pale green skin showed.

But that was not the only difference.

They had a more relaxed demeanour. No longer were they huddled together, apprehensive, suspicious; each stood confidently apart from the rest, huge eyes glistening, an expression on their face that was almost a smile.

Brog shook Jed who snuffled himself awake just as the Leader spoke in the booming voice so incompatible with his size: "Yooooo mayyyyyyk thhhhhe Sooooooouuuurce strrooooonng," he bellowed, and waved his pincer hand in a gesture of well-being.

His attendants all nodded vigorously, and clacked their pincers in an obvious sign of approval.

"Thhhhe Soooooouurce issss nooo looonnn-ger cooooool."

Indeed, if anything, the chamber floor was getting hotter, as Jed pointed out as they rose stiffly to their feet.

Brog addressed the Leader of the Guardians.

"The Source is not yet repaired," he explained, knowing as he did so that as far as the Guardians were concerned, the problem had been solved. They had their heat back.

"Thhhhe Soooouuurrce isss noooowww strooooonnng," insisted the Leader.

"Mooooooooore strooooonnng!" came the chorus from his attendants, "stroooooonng and mooooore strooooonng!" and they all clacked and nodded, nodded and clacked, touching pincers together in quite a congratulatory way.

"*Too* strong," said Jed aside to Brog, shuffling uncomfortably as the heat built beneath his feet.

The orange glow had a hint of yellow about it now, and sweat beads were beginning to break out on their faces.

The Guardians were almost dancing with delight, but Brog was anxious, and looking across at Jed, he knew it was shared.

"The heat is building," he said, and Jed nodded.

"As though it has no outlet, no escape."

"With the Disc jammed, where can it go?"

The probability struck them simultaneously.

With the Disc unable to provide an outlet for the energy pouring from the Source beam, that energy was accumulating, feeding back across the Valley of Light, through the tunnels in the Mountains of Separation. It was evident that sooner or later the energy level was going to exceed the capacity of the ground to contain it, and when that happened . . .

Brog turned to the Leader.

"Show us the way from the tunnels," he said, and there was urgency in his voice.

The Leader scanned Brog and Jed's anxious faces, looked to his attendants, happy, relaxed, and finally to the floor, which he leaned down and felt with his one hand. As he did so, a trickle of perspiration ran down his cheek and dropped to the ground; he dipped a finger into it curiously.

When he straightened, he turned a face to them that was not as content as it had been moments before.

"Aaaaall issss nooooot weeeeell," he mouthed laboriously.

"No," echoed Brog, "all is not well. We must reach the Source across the Valley."

The attendants had stopped rejoicing, one or two were showing signs of discomfort. Eventually they stood, looking uneasy, sensing the disquiet generated by their Leader.

"Coooommme," he blared, and turning, tottered away on his short, stumpy legs.

Thankful and apprehensive, Brog and Jed followed him.

CHAPTER 24

Throughout the Blacktime, the Gork had kept up a relentless search for the Stoop who had stolen their eggs.

Klan's plan was working well so far, and the raiding parties who had stolen the eggs had led the Gork as near to the Glowurld as possible, taunting them with glimpses of the eggs they carried, occasionally goading them into a frenzy by smashing an egg before their eyes – a move guaranteed to enrage the Gork, and draw them even further from the Darkness.

Whilst this was going on, the remainder of the Stoopwarriors had left the Sheerstone, some had joined the egg-raiders, others had crept around and behind the pursuing Gork, and now were stretched the whole length of the border between the Great Gloom and the Darkness.

Hundreds of them, armed with throwstiks and Ka'thuks, lay like a living barrier between the Gork and their safeplace, their task to delay the retreat of the Gork once the Light had been restored.

Like the others, they had no idea just when, or even if, that might happen.

While there had been Light, the odds against the Stoop had been considerable, but manageable. Their greater mobility had kept them out of the clutches of the Gork. However, now that the Blacktime was here, the Gork had been reinforced by many members of the OldBreed, more used to the Blackhours than their younger counterparts, experienced in prowling the dark Gloom as they had done for generations, seeking out and killing.

In addition, the lack of Light hampered the essence of the plan, for no longer could the Stoop taunt their enemy with sight of the eggs.

So, the Stoop took to the hollows.

Not to regenerate, as their instincts told them they should, but to survive, for the open ground, in the Blackhours, in the Great Gloom was, *this* Blacktime, more of a death trap than it had ever been.

And yet they could not afford to hide too well, could not afford the risk that the Gork would tire of the hunt and return to the Darkness. Now that they had been lured from their safe-place, they had to be kept there for as long as it took Brog to restore the Light – or failing that, until the last Stoop had fought himself to a standstill.

They say a Stoop is born knowing how to dig a hollow, and a major part of that vital construction is the camouflage that conceals it from an enemy.

This was the reason that the Stoop nation had existed so long despite nightly raids from the Darkness.

To a predator, a hollow must be invisible, and on that Blacktime when every Gork in the Drab-wurld was hunting the egg, never were hollows more carefully constructed or better disguised. So well disguised, that the Gork were left with the impossible task of having to tear up every single tree in order to find them, and there were simply too many trees for that.

Each Stoop took it upon himself to harass the enemy, creeping out whenever it seemed quiet overhead, flitting like ghosts from hollow to hollow, taunting, howling, throwing stones or fallen branches, then melting out of sight, always taking care not to give away the location of a hollow, which could contain as many as eight Stoop.

Klan was amongst the most daring and effective of these Blacktime raiders, scarcely ever in a hollow at all, darting around, a bundle of throwstiks across his shoulder, stopping now and then to hurl one in the direction of a clumsy noise, and hitting his mark on a surprising number of occasions. But not every Stoop had Klan's skills, or the luck needed to evade an enemy time after time, and that long, long Blacktime, more than one Stoop left his hollow and did not return.

Pik had made sure that Kora was safely ensconced in a hollow on the edges of the Glowurld, one less likely to be discovered due to its remote position, before slipping off into the Blackness to play his part in the fight. Now, several incidents later, mud-splattered and panting, and with a need for more throwstiks, he could only guess at which part of the Great Gloom he was in.

A clumsy shuffling to his left caused him to turn; it was immediately followed by a similar sound directly behind him. He had no need to see to know that there were Gork near, very near indeed. The fetid smell had already reached his nostrils, and their feeble attempts to move quietly meant that they had located him.

For a moment he considered which threat he might meet first, ahead or behind, and then a third option presented itself.

His experienced eye saw signs of a hollow not two leaps off, and quickly, carefully, and not until he was as sure as he could be that he could not be seen, he lifted the camouflage moss and slid into it, leaving two more bewildered Gork to wonder where their prey had vanished.

Lin sheathed her claws as she recognized the arrival of a fellow Stoop, and smiled broadly when she saw that it was Pik. He was glad of the water and muskbread she was able to offer him, and replenished his stock of throwstiks from the pile that were there.

There were three other Stoop in the hollow, all taking a brief rest from their efforts, and piled in a corner, a dull, yellow-grey sheen on their pitted surface, lay two large Gork eggs.

"How goes the Blacktime?" asked a Stoop.

"Slowly," replied Pik, "the slowest I can remember." He wiped the sweat from his face. "How is the action in this part?"

"Not good," was the reply. "In the early hours many Gork were overhead, now there seem few. It could be the Gork tire of the chase."

Lin chipped in. "Not while they know we have their eggs."

Pik considered. "They know we *took* their eggs," he said finally.

"Is that not the same?" asked another Stoop.

Pik shook his head. "If they believe the eggs have been destroyed, that the chance has been lost to recover them, yes, they may return to the Darkness."

"That will kill the Plan, we must keep them here until full Light returns!"

"If it returns," put in another.

Lin's eyes blazed. "If it is possible, Brog will do it!"

Pik raised a hand to calm matters. "The Lord Klan has taken a calculated risk," he said, and his voice carried the confidence he felt in his Leader. "Whether the Light returns, or no, the decision to draw the Gork from the Darkness has been made – we must carry it through."

The others nodded agreement.

Lin broke the silence which followed.

"But if the Gork *do* feel their eggs cannot be retrieved . . ."

Pik smiled and crept over to where the eggs lay. "Then we must convince· them that the search is still worthwhile . . ." he said.

Less than a hundred breaths later, one Gork egg lay in the clearing above Lin's hollow.

Pik and the other three Stoopwarriors lay

hidden in the surrounding undergrowth, throw-stiks loaded into slings, eyes enlarged in the watery moonlight.

"Remember," Pik whispered to them, "we must allow one to escape with the egg."

"It binds me that we must," muttered one of them.

"It is a sacrifice worth making," put in another, "as the word spreads that an egg has been found . . ."

He got no further, for at that moment the sound of breaking branches reached their ears, and they tensed behind their cover.

Three Gork broke out into the clearing, line abreast, OldBreeds, beating the bushes with their tails, sweeping the trees with their hate-filled gaze. All three stopped dead as they saw the egg, the luminosity of the shell standing out in the moonlight.

One turned immediately and stormed off into the Treelands, his head thrown back as he uttered a low-pitched howling to alert others in the vicinity. The other two darted forward, one picked up the egg, and both were on the verge of following their companion when the Stoop sprang their ambush. They targeted the Gork without the egg and in seconds he lay writhing on the ground, no less than four throwstiks skewering his upper chest, another thudding into his throat as he lay there. The other raced away, the egg clutched tightly in his claws.

Pik nodded his satisfaction. "Soon, for each tree about here, there will be two Gork."

He stood back as his three friends slipped, one by one, into the hollow. He would have followed them, but one quick look around caused him to hesitate, the moss held up by one corner.

From the bushes, he caught a movement, less than a fractional change in the shape of a tree, and he knew that he was being watched.

Gradually, he lowered the camouflage, and eased the end of a throwstik into his sling. A second's hesitation, and he flung the stik in the direction of the watcher.

At the same moment, the figure moved and the stik hit the tree with a mighty thwack, the resonance echoing in the woods. The bush erupted, and the Gork who had raised the alarm on finding the egg burst out and charged at Pik with a full-blooded roar.

Pik knew he had to draw the creature from the hollow and kill it too, for if it killed him it would return for the others.

He dodged its first charge, ran across the clearing, and full into a thick, low tree branch, the blow stunning him.

The Gork saw his chance and lunged. Pik's

head swam, the roar of the Gork filled his ears, then . . . silence.

As his vision cleared, he saw that the Gork lay on its back, limp and lifeless. A Stoop foot was on its chest, and a blond Magnawood Ka'thuk was being drawn from its heart.

Pik realized that for the second time in the last few Dayspans he had reason to thank his Stooplord for his life.

"It is a long, long Blacktime," said Klan, casually.

CHAPTER 25

The tunnel entrance out of which Brog and Pik emerged from the Mountains of Separation, into the Valley of Light led straight onto the Valley floor, and Brog left it at a run.

Jed's leg injury, they had agreed, could not be allowed to dictate the speed at which they moved.

Jed watched him go, wondering, as he sped off, if it would be the last time he would see his friend.

The odds against Brog were great indeed; the odds against him actually being able to restore the Light were practically non-existent, but while there was even a slim chance, he had to try. The alternative was becoming plainer to see by the hour, as the Light and heat beneath the surface of the floor began to build to a point at which it would erupt.

Jed watched Brog go, then limped after him as fast as his injury would allow, leaving the tunnel entrance to the group of Guardians who had led them there, their hairless green faces plainly showing the anxiety they felt, their Leader subdued, watching the receding figure of Jed, and the speck in the distance that was Brog.

The whole Valley was lit from below, the eerie glow coating each boulder, each hillock in a butter-yellow light, throwing the top half into shadow. The fine, dry dust billowed up in Brog's wake as he hurtled over the ground, eyes behind the eyeshield narrowed to slits against the glare from the floor, his blond mane streaming out behind him as he put his whole strength into his effort, legs a blur of movement.

If it hadn't been for the threat it posed, the sight of the floodlit Valley would have been beautiful to behold, as the glow crept up the sides of the mountains before fading into the black void above.

Brog's mind raced ahead to his arrival at the Mound of Extremes. What would he find?

Redeye's sight would not have been affected

as much as Brog's, for even though Brog wore the eyeshield, Redeye had the advantage of being further from the glare of the Valley floor. Redeye must know that he was trapped and doomed to die, and Brog could not imagine such a monster accepting that easily.

It was not in Redeye's nature to sacrifice himself for the good of his tribe, and Brog knew that the Gork would be anxious to save his own skin if he could.

In order to cross to the plinth which held the Disc from the spot where the path ended, Brog would have to rely, once again, on help from Planimal, and as Brog's strong legs ate the ground, and the Mound of Extremes drew rapidly closer, he turned his thoughts to the little plant-animal and tried to make mind-contact with him.

"Planimal," he hissed through clenched teeth, "where are you, my friend? I need you now!"

But no thoughts or images came back to him; no indication that his transmental message was being picked up, and as the heat began to build up from the Valley floor, Brog redoubled his efforts, his mind pumping his friend's name into the atmosphere in rhythm with his stride:

"Plani-mal . . . Plani-mal . . . Plani-mal . . ."

It wasn't until he got much nearer to the Mound that he felt the contact, and received the first mental images from Planimal. The images grew stronger with each leap he covered, so that, by the time he found himself within five hundred leaps of the Mound's base, he knew that he was no longer alone in his task, that whatever help Planimal could give, he *would* give.

Brog lost precious time in locating the Glo-keeper's path. He had approached the Mound from a different direction, and didn't know if the path lay to his left or his right.

He chose to go to the left, skirting the Mound's perimeter, his tired eyes searching the writhing, churning surface for signs of the narrow strip which would lead him upwards, before finally, deciding he had gone far enough, he turned to search in the other direction.

Immediately he did so, a vine from the Mound's surface threw itself into his path, to be followed by another . . . and another. Brog's surprise melted into realization as Planimal's mischievous face leapt into his subconscious, and turning once again, he continued his search in the same direction. Not ten leaps on, there, stark and hard against the turbulent background, lay the path he sought.

The journey up the path was more difficult than before. The surface of Extremes was far more agitated than it had been, almost as though the build-up of pressure and heat beneath it was irritating the organisms responsible for the phenomenon.

Determinedly, Brog fought, dodged, and manoeuvred his way along the narrow strip, deafened by the noise.

As he neared the rim of the plateau, his luck left him temporarily. He had just swayed to his right to avoid the upthrust of a spike-leaved bush, when a Magnawood sapling emerged from the surface by his left shoulder; as it snaked across his back, the leaves sprouting and crumbling progressively, a branch shot out and hooked the eyeshield from his face.

Brog snatched at the air, desperate to retrieve it, but could only watch in dismay as it was thrown far away and sank beneath the volatile mass.

Luckily, the Light level at the time of his loss was not fierce enough to affect him, but his spirits sank, and he felt that his already slim chances had been greatly diminished.

After what seemed a lifetime, his head drew level with the plateau rim, and he cautiously peered over the edge to where the plinth lay, holding its massive burden.

He saw the wedge of stone with which Redeye had jammed the Disc, but of Redeye himself there was no sign.

Moving as stealthily as his precarious surroundings would allow, Brog heaved himself
over the edge and, breath held, expecting
Redeye to appear from around the edge of the
Disc at any moment, he covered the stretch as
far as the gap where the path ran out.

Even before he got there, he could see the
vines and plants around the edge beginning to
move in unison, and recognized that Planimal
was exerting his influence on them.

Within the space of a few heartbeats, they
had writhed and woven themselves into a living
mat, strong and supple enough to take Brog's
weight.

As Brog watched it form, crossing and re-
crossing itself, plaiting its innumerable strands,
he took time to gather his thoughts.

Unless Redeye was already dead, which was
unlikely, for the plinth was a considerable
sanctuary in the ocean of confusion which
surrounded it, then Brog, once he had crossed
the mat of vines, was going to find himself
trapped there with his deadly enemy, and strong
though he was, he was going to need more than
strength to match Redeye, the killer of his
mother; Redeye, the butcher of his people;
Redeye, the destroyer of Light.

Suddenly, his hatred for the giant seemed
to reach its peak. The events of the last few

Dayspans reran themselves in his mind, all the suffering caused by Redeye's greed and evil descended on him like a weight, and fired a great anger which burned deep in his chest.

He drew his Ka'thuk, held it upright and pressed the flat of the blade to his forehead in the traditional salute to all those who had perished, then deliberately, he drew the keen edge across the back of his arm, watching as the blood flowed from the shallow cut, a symbolic gesture, performed through the ages by those about to fight until the death.

He strode swiftly across the carpet of vines and leapt nimbly onto the plinth.

Coiled for split-second reaction, legs spread to counter his balance, he eased his way to the edge of the Disc and peered around it, looking along its thick edge.

Seeing nothing, he rounded the edge, back pressed to it, and shuffled warily along to peer around the other side. If Redeye still lived, this was where he was going to be found, along the other face of the Disc. There was nowhere else that he could hide.

Slowly, Brog leaned forward, and shot a one-eyed look along the Disc face.

There was nothing there!

A wave of relief flooded him. What could it mean?

There was no way that Redeye could have escaped from the plinth alive; the trapdoor was too small for him to enter, besides, the Light down there would have killed him instantly. Had he fallen (or jumped) into the surface of Extremes? Did this mean that all Brog's worries were over? That all he had to do was remove the stone which jammed the Disc to relieve the pressure? That, at least, would restore the Light to its subdued level, give him and Jed time to work on some sort of repair.

He slipped the sword into his belt, and turned, just as, with a roar like a thunderclap, Redeye leapt from his perch high up on the Disc, and dropped like a stone, to land squarely on hind paws not a body length away.

The heavy spikeball ripped a groove along Brog's chest before biting deep into the edge of the Disc.

Brog's reaction was just as quick. Drawing and swinging his blade in one continuous move-ment, he struck a sweeping blow which caught Redeye unawares. It was the flat of Brog's sword which hit Redeye's wrist; the edge would have taken the clawed hand off, but as it happened, the contact numbed the limb so that the chain on the spikeball slipped from his nerveless claws.

As the ball fell, it rolled along the plinth and over the edge, dragging the chain with it.

Brog turned and ran along the face of the Disc, needing space in which to face his enemy, space which really didn't exist in the circumstances, but at least here he would be able to retreat a step at a time if he had to, and make Redeye fight for any advance he might make.

He turned as Redeye swung into view around the Disc edge, saliva dripping from the green and broken teeth bordering his ugly, red, gaping jaws, tiny eyes burning with evil intent.

He advanced, hesitating as he passed the woven vines, and for one moment Brog thought he might attempt a crossing to the path, but he only leered his intentions, which plainly were to kill Brog first and make good his escape later.

He moved with confidence now, like a predator upon a helpless victim, his attitude one of almost disbelief that the Stoop should deliver himself *and* a means of escape.

With little need to rush, he advanced arrogantly, keeping an eye on the point of Brog's sword, until at last, he was invading the space that Brog occupied.

Brog lunged a half dozen times, cutting the Gork deeply on four occasions about the arms, and the thick green blood spattered the Disc.

Enraged, Redeye swept his razor claws a

finger width from Brog's face, and received a stab to the leg for his trouble.

Redeye stood back and surveyed the situation. This Stoop was quick and clever. He had to dispose of him more rapidly than he would have wished. A little suffering would have been nice, but under the circumstances . . .

With a speed that took Brog by surprise, Redeye swung his tail.

Brog saw it coming only at the last moment, and although he managed to step back from it, the tip caught his Ka'thuk and smashed it against the Disc, from where it rebounded to land plumb in the centre of the mat of vines, and well out of reach.

Redeye threw back his head and roared in triumph. Perhaps a little suffering *was* possible now.

Unarmed as he was, Brog had no choice but to back away as slowly as Redeye advanced.

Looking around desperately for something, anything, with which to defend himself, he saw only the rock which he and Jed had used to plug the hole to block the beam of escaping Light.

Too heavy to lift . . . and then an idea began to form.

Purposely, Brog backed towards the rock as though he hadn't seen it, mentally preparing himself for the acting performance of his life; if the plan was to work he would now have to convince Redeye that he was terrified.

Redeye followed him, snarling, savouring the moment when he would strike, taking pleasure from the helplessness of his victim. As he watched, the Stoop stumbled over a rock and fell flat on his back, the fear contorting his face.

Redeye had seen that look of fear many times before, and it always gave him a feeling of elation. It was the moment that he knew well, when the victim was finally his to do with as he wanted.

As he moved in for the slow kill, the Stoop, in sheer desperation, reached for the rock he had fallen over – and attempted to lift it!

Redeye roared his version of a laugh.

The rock was obviously too heavy, and yet the terrified creature had tried to throw it at him! How desperate some of them became just before they died.

How should this one die?

Should he be torn to pieces? Stamped to death? He smirked at the pitiful way in which the Stoop still tried to lift the rock. If he could, the Stoop would kill him with that rock. Why not let the rock kill the Stoop?

The idea appealed to him.

He growled his pleasure. Yes! . . . now was

the moment . . . now. He bent, placed his two great clawed hands on the rock and lifted it effortlessly from the depression in which it lay.

Brog never actually saw what happened next, he turned his face away, closed his eyes tight and covered them with his hands.

CHAPTER 26

Ted had seen the ray of pure Light shoot into the sky as he had approached the Mound, and knew that something significant had happened, though he could only guess (and worry) about what it might be.

His walk across the Valley had seemed to ease, rather than aggravate his injury, and he had been able, after a while, to break into a trot, feeding his weight gradually onto the damaged muscle, hoping that the exercise would firm it up. Now, as he arrived at the foot of the Mound of Extremes, apart from a little throbbing, the limb felt more functional than it had done since the accident.

He was anxious to get to Brog.

In a one-to-one situation, even Brog was no match for the giant. At least with two of them the odds would be a little better.

Brog's three-toed prints were clear to see in the dust, and Jed followed them round to where the path began to snake up across the churning, volatile surface of Extremes.

Looking upwards, he could still see the ray of Light stabbing the black of the sky like a living knife, and he wondered again about its sudden appearance.

Brog would not have been able to move that rock alone, but Redeye would have no reason to move it.

With a dread in his heart, he began the perilous climb.

The sight that met Jed's gaze as he peered cautiously over the rim of the plateau at the end of his climb momentarily stopped his heart.

Redeye lay as he had fallen, on his back, one arm hanging over the plinth, his horrible head turned to one side, eyes staring in fright, his huge mouth open in a frozen scream, teeth bared and tongue hanging.

Jed ducked.

It was only after a second, wary look that it began to dawn on him that the monster was perhaps in no position to pose a threat. Following swiftly on the heels of that discovery came the realization that Redeye was very dead indeed.

But where was Brog?

Crawling the rest of the way along the path, Jed spotted the Ka'thuk, the one thing that his friend was not likely to have parted with if he could help it.

Redeye was dead, but had he slain Brog before dying?

"Brog!" called Jed, but his voice was drowned by the noise around him.

"Brog!" But there was no reply.

Nimbly, he skipped across the mat of vines, instinctively avoiding the Gork's body, repulsed even now by the evil it represented, onto the plinth.

He saw the slab of stone wedging the Disc, heard the groan as the Disc tried to turn, without success.

Brog was nowhere to be seen on this side of the Disc, and Jed turned, to round the corner and look there.

Brog was sitting with his back against the Disc edge, a strip of cloth from his waist tied around his eyes, legs straight out in front of him. The livid spikeball wound across his chest had congealed, but not before the blood had covered his lower abdomen, and Jed's first reaction was that Brog was dead.

Jed *had* been wrong before, and this turned out to be one of those times as, with a start, Brog's head twitched towards the sound of Jed's arrival, and realizing his friend was there, he angled his head, a weary smile on his face.

Jed took in the inflamed cheeks, the wound, the battle-weariness, and gained some impression of the ordeal that Brog had been through.

He knelt, looked into the Stoop's face, a face he knew he would remember with affection for the rest of his life, no matter how divided their lives might be from now on.

He laid Brog's sword across his friend's knees.

"You dropped this," he said, simply.

Brog fondled the blade, gripped his friend's wrist. Slowly, a grin spread across his face, and the two of them did something they had not done together before – they laughed.

The Source beam had hit Redeye right between the eyes, killing him.

It had also averted (for the time being, at least) the danger of a pressure build-up, and the Valley floor had begun to take on a darker colour once again.

The great Disc was straining to turn, its black segments staring out like eyeless sockets, maintaining a Blacktime already much longer than usual.

The priority now was to find a way of repairing the Source, a way in which the beam could be directed once more onto the hub of the Disc.

It seemed an impossible task, particularly since Brog's eyes had to remain covered whilst the beam was escaping. Even a glance at it could prove as fatal to him as it had been to Redeye.

"We must block the hole again," said Jed, "remove the wedge, let the Disc turn."

Brog nodded resignedly, the soreness around the bandage covering his eyes apparent.

Jed spoke more low. "How will you survive the Light?"

Brog took a breath before replying. "I won't," he said, "but that is my problem. The Source must be repaired."

They sat for a long time, their backs to the Source beam, shielded from it by the bulk of the Disc, putting forward different theories, each proving impossible to execute given the circumstances in which they found themselves.

On one thing they were agreed, the Source beam had to be diverted . . .

"Like a stream, to flow in a different direction," Jed observed.

Brog nodded thoughtfully. "Like a stream," he muttered. "Sometimes, in the Great Gloom, the Light dances in the trees wherever there is a stream. It bounces from the surface of the water."

"May it always do so," said Jed, idly, the significance of the remark evading him.

"Do you not see?" queried Brog. "We must do the same. We must bounce the Source so that it falls on the centre of the Disc."

"With . . . with *water*?"

"With whatever will turn the Light to shine in the direction we wish," gabbled Brog, excited now.

He risked his eyes to lift the bandage just enough to enable him to draw in the dust with a stone.

"See?" he explained. "The Disc is here . . . the beam must be made to shine across to here . . . and from here . . . onto the Disc . . ."

He stopped suddenly, looked at the stone in his hand, turning it, felt the smoothness, noting how the glow from the beam overhead was reflected from the surface.

"What is it?" Jed enquired.

Brog showed what he had in his hand.

"A stone?" said Jed.

"Not a stone," replied Brog.

"What then?"

Brog caught his eye, an incredulous note creeping into his voice. "A scale!"

Jed looked more closely and picked up another from the ground.

"A scale from Redeye! When I hit his arm he must have lost them! See, Jed! See how they shine!"

"Like the surface of a stream!"

"And Jed," continued Brog, elated, "his body is covered in them!"

It was Jed who got the job of hacking off the opalescent scales from Redeye's chest, a job he did with trepidation, his imagination running riot, every moment expecting the dead Gork to rise up. He transported the scales to the far side of the Disc where Brog worked feverishly, beating them together using a smooth rock and sometimes the hilt of his sword.

It was back-breaking work, but piece by piece, little by little, the first of the two reflective dishes they would need to divert the route of the Source beam began to take shape.

Bending the beaten scales over a hump of rock, Brog pounded the surface until his hands bled, welding the metallic scales together to form a concavity, his sweat mingling with the oily resin which oozed from the joints where each scale overlapped.

In a comparatively short time, they had a dish

about the size of two handspans and, learning from their mistakes with the first one, they took less time to complete the second.

If the idea was to work, it would be the greatest of ironies that the very creature whose sole intention had been to extinguish the Light for ever should play a vital part in returning the Light to its full power, and it was this thought, as much as anything else, which drove them on with such vigour.

Ripping a length of cloth from his waist, Jed gave the dishes a final polish, until the beaten scales shone as brightly as the surface of any stream.

"It will work?" he asked, anxiously.

"We have only to try it to know."

Jed hesitated, preferring for the moment to hold onto the hope they both felt, rather than risk the failure of this, their only chance.

"If it is to work we will know instantly," said Brog, "if not – then we will have tried our best."

The trial had to be Jed's responsibility, and he began by approaching the escaping Source beam, the dish held before his face for protection, and placing the dish over the escape hole.

In the comparative blackness which followed, he jammed it in place with rock, and groped his way back, past Redeye's body, to where Brog was enjoying blessed relief from the glare.

He had to wait until his eyes became accustomed to the dark, before the Valley floor below, with its red glow, slowly swam into his vision.

With the Source once again trapped inside the chamber, it would not be long before that redness began to increase in intensity, and Jed turned dutifully to the second and most difficult part of the trial.

Brog could only wait in apprehension, eyes bandaged, as Jed opened the trapdoor, his own sword through the ring-pull providing the leverage. The brilliance which forced its way out from the opening in a long, square beam far exceeded that which had shone from the escape-hole.

Brog buried his face in his hands as Jed, with a moment's respite to allow his half-closed eyes to accustom themselves to the glare, stepped through the hole, the second dish tucked under his arm.

Long before he reached the bottom of the steps, he could see that the diverted beam was playing full upon the back wall of the chamber, more or less opposite the centre of the Disc. Shielding his eyes as much as he could, and ignoring the stabbing pain that was beginning to invade his head, he reached high and caught the beam in the dish.

Immediately, the beam was diverted and shot

about the chamber like a searchlight, amplifying any movement Jed made, dancing wildly around, leaving an after-trail in its wake as it careered madly, like something alive.

Bringing his arms under control, Jed found he could direct the beam quite easily, and lost no time in swinging it over to where the Disc stood, its transparent hub jutting out just below the surface of the high roof.

Jed held his breath.

This was the moment of truth.

What would happen if the idea didn't work? If the Source beam was, perhaps, weakened by being diverted along two different angles?

Slowly, he played the Light across the wall, onto the Disc, across its three remaining black segments, then quickly – suddenly anxious to know the result – onto the hub.

Brog, with his back against the edge of the Disc, felt the sudden jolt and heard the deep whine as the Disc jarred violently against the wedge, striving like a Goliath to turn as it had turned since time began.

With a crack which echoed out across the Valley of Light, the slab of stone jamming it burst into a thousand fragments as the Disc moved.

Jed laid the dish on the floor, allowing the beam to play once more on the wall behind him, and ran like a demon up the steps.

Brog was on his back, the tears of relief saturating the bandage across his eyes as Jed stuck his head through the opening.

"Yaaaaahhhh-hhheeeeehhhh!" he screamed. "Brog! We've done it!"

He sprang from the hole, threw himself upon his friend, and they rolled, joyously, from side to side, each slapping the other's back, sobs and laughter mingling as the sheer enormity of their achievement sank in.

As soon as Jed was able to fix the second dish permanently in place, and the remaining black segments had been allowed to roll around, a Dayspan would begin which Brog had not seen since he was a Stoopling.

But exposure to it would certainly kill him.

CHAPTER 27

The Gork teemed through the Great Gloom like ants.

OldBreed and NewBreed alike rampaged in their thousands through the Treelands, ranging out into the Glowurld, drunk with a success that made them reckless.

The Blacktime had stretched on and on, and it was obvious to them now that Redeye had extinguished the Light for ever – the whole Terrawurld was theirs for the taking.

No longer would their hunting and killing be restricted to the darker corners of the Great Gloom. Now they could range far and wide, into the Uplands, the Far and Mid-regions, out into the Glowurld and beyond, and find other victims, other tribes, to devour.

In the first few hours of their new freedom, they scavenged, pirate-like, unable to believe their good fortune, into areas previously denied them, spoiling, destroying, not even hunting for Stoop, knowing that the Stoop could be hunted and killed at their leisure, almost as a pastime.

They poured from the Darkness, every last one of them, greedily anxious to claim all that they saw, all that their black hearts desired.

For the Stoop in the hollows, in the Sheerstone, and those guarding the border of the Darkness to delay any retreat, there was nothing but despondency.

Already exhausted through prolonged activity in the Blacktime, unable to regenerate their cells, the first twinges of doubt about the Light had begun when the time for the new Dayspan had approached, and still the Gork of the Old-Breed had made no attempt to retreat to the Darkness. From then, the hopes of the Stoop had faded in direct proportion to the increasing elation of the Gork.

In every hollow sat Stoop with bowed heads, many tearful, weeping not for themselves, but for the lost freedom of their nation, for the Wurld that their Stooplings would never know, and for their beloved Great Gloom, now being ravaged and abused by a worthless, evil enemy.

In Lin's hollow, only Klan kept his regal composure, the disappointment hidden behind a mask of defiance, unable, even had he wished, to give in.

Lin's sadness was twofold: she felt as much as anybody else the loss of the long, long battle, tasted as everybody else did the bitterness of defeat, but it also meant for her that she was denied even the comfort of spending her last remaining hours with the one she loved, for the loss of the Light surely meant that Brog was dead.

She looked across to Klan, knowing that it was his loss too, and with a heavy heart she went over, sat beside him, and laid a weary head on his broad shoulder.

Overhead, the crashing and roaring continued, and each minute that passed hung heavier on the hearts of all who heard it.

A Stoop is a creature with a love of life, a love of freedom, and a deep pride in all that he does.

When that freedom to live has been taken away, and when the very thing that they hold most precious, the right to live in their own way amongst the things they love, has been destroyed, then there can only be one outcome.

Already each Stoop had decided that, rather

than spend the rest of their days in hiding, they would prefer to die fighting. All that they were waiting for as they sat in the scattered hollows or in the Sheerstone, was for their Stooplord to give the signal which would send every Stoop, Stoopette and Stoopling out into the Treelands to fight to the death.

Once begun, they knew there could be no half-measures, no retreats, no respite, and each knew that there could be only one end result – the extermination of the Stoop people.

Against such massive odds, and in conditions which favoured their enemy, they could not hope to win, but it was far better to die fighting than to live like trapped and hunted animals in a land no longer their own.

In the hollow where he waited, Klan slowly came to his feet. He drew himself to his full height, the light of defiance glinting in his eyes, the long, blond mane cascading around his shoulders, and Pik, seeing him, could only gasp at his resemblance to Brog.

Klan drew the razor-sharp Ka'thuk from his belt, balanced the grip firmly in his hand, and looked around the small group of warriors there with him.

"It is time," he said, quietly, "time for the Stoop to show what being Stoop means."

Every eye was upon him.

"Time for us to fight for all that is worth fighting for, all that is worth dying for."

Lin held back her tears, raised her chin proudly at the words. All over the Great Gloom now, Stoop would be readying themselves, saying their last goodbyes to loved ones, preparing to sell their lives dearly.

"We have fought a good fight," Klan continued, "fought for the things we hold dear. For generations, since time began, we have lived as we live. Now we can live no longer – let us show the Gork how we can die!"

And turning, he pushed up through the camouflage into the damp, black air, followed by Pik, Lin and the handful who had been privileged to listen to his last words.

He strode to the centre of the clearing, spread his feet, ceremoniously drew blood from his forearm, then threw back his head and sent a roar ringing through the trees which caused the very branches to rattle.

As the battlecry spread over the Great Gloom, every Gork stopped dead in his tracks, and a shiver ran down each and every cowardly spine.

The cry drifted to the Uplands, to Planimal as he stood by Brog's old hollow, and he swayed anxiously backwards and forwards on his slender stem.

Standing on his balcony overlooking the crater, the Drabkeeper heard it and beat a clenched fist into his open palm as it echoed faintly around the crater walls.

The cry echoed out across the Glowurld, to where the Humans were rebuilding the Palace of the Glokeeper, and they laid down their tools and exchanged fearful glances.

Every Stoop heard it, and it fired them with purpose.

Like a swarm of angry bees, from scores of hollows, from the rockholes of the Sheerstone, from all parts of the region, they emerged, fighting as they came, and the last, bloody battle of the Great Gloom began.

The awesome ferocity of the Stoop attack, from all places at once, took the Gork completely by surprise, and the first half hour of the battle saw them suffer dreadful losses. Pik, with Lin at his side, had fought his way through to where Kora was, and the three of them now stood, shoulder to shoulder, Ka'thuks whistling and thrusting, the two Stoopettes fighting as ferociously as any warrior, their hatred fired by the memory of their Moonruns of captivity.

Klan was a tower of inspiration to all who saw him. So fierce was his onslaught that the bodies of the Gork he slew lay piled around him, and several Gork ran rather than face his sword.

During that Blacktime, many Stoop discovered their true courage, and found new strength time and again, fighting savagely, with a vigour born of determination, with nothing to lose but the lives which they were doomed to lose anyway, united in their efforts by a desire to defend, to the last drop of blood, the homeland they loved.

By comparison, the Gork were united in nothing, shared nothing except the greed which had always been their trademark.

Disorganized, undisciplined, without pity or feeling, they could afford to sacrifice large numbers of their own kind, and gradually, through sheer weight of numbers, because for every Gork killed there was always another to take his place, they began to force themselves upon the tired but determined Stoop.

The tide of battle began to turn, and despite the Herculean efforts of Klan and the others, the Stoop began to fall back towards the Sheerstone, where they would make their last stand.

It was then that a moment arrived which would be talked about in Stooplore for generations.

Over the whole battleground, every Gork of the OldBreed stopped and turned a fearful head towards the Glowurld.

For one long moment there was total confusion, and the Stoop were able to rally, the pressure temporarily relieved, then . . . panic! Each OldBreed broke off the attack and scurried desperately in the direction of the Darkness.

Hardly daring to believe what they saw, even less reluctant to hope what the action might mean, the Stoop pressed their advantage against an enemy which seemed, suddenly, to have lost the desire to fight.

The NewBreed were looking anxiously about them, half-heartedly defending themselves, unsure, puzzled, afraid.

It was Klan who recognized first what was happening.

With an exultant cry, he rallied a group of warriors and ran to a point where they could intercept the fleeing Gork and cut them off from the Darkness they were so anxious to reach.

Another moment, and the reason for their panic became apparent to all, as, far out over the Glowurld, appeared the first, faint crack of Light which was to herald a new Dayspan.

Stunned to silence, the NewBreed gazed at the lightening sky, while the OldBreed made frenzied attempts to breach the blockade that Klan had thrown across their paths; one or two broke through, but were brought down by throwstiks, and then, quite suddenly, for them it was all over.

As the Light spread rapidly across the sky, the Stoop cries of delight hit the air like a wave, and the OldBreed began to fall, writhing in agony, their limbs flailing to a standstill as death overtook them.

The NewBreed had lost the will to fight, and any onlooker might have thought that the Stoop had, also. In reality, both sides were faced with a prospect far more important to either of them than even a fight to the death.

Gork and Stoop alike stood transfixed, frozen in action, side by side, the silence so complete that it could almost be heard, as they stared through the trees at the sky above the Glowurld. Even those wounded on the ground forgot their injuries and gazed open-mouthed at the ever-brightening sky.

Would the Light level still be weak? Or had Brog, son of Klan, achieved what he had set out to do – to restore the Light to its full strength?

The silence, the waiting, became unbearable.

Then, from the direction of the Glowurld, from those Gork out there with no trees for protection, came the screams that told the tale, as they fell, dead, on the barren surface.

Gone was the feeble, watery wash of Light with which each span had begun since the great ground-shake; this was a brilliant, bold, vivid, refreshing beginning to the new day, a span which promised to be as spans used to be, and Klan led the cheering as it filtered through the trees, giving the glow to the Great Gloom so sadly missed.

In every direction, Gork were dropping as the Light struck them. Those who covered their eyes lasted only moments longer.

Everywhere, Stoop were rejoicing, hugging, dancing in delight, weeping in relief, shouting with joy, kneeling, arms raised, letting the blessed Light fall upon them.

From somewhere, a Stoop set up a chant, and gradually it spread across the Treelands until every Stoop was voicing it:

"Brog!... Brog!... Brog!... Brog!... Brog!"

At the height of the euphoria, a four-bladed Gork spear came hurtling from a dark area on the borders of the Darkness, thrown in a last desperate effort, by a dying Gork.

It buried itself deep in the back of Klan the Golden.

He died at the height of his happiness.

CHAPTER 28

Brog peered through red and swollen eyes at the plate of food that Jed had brought him.

In the soothing dimness of the thick-walled room, he had had time to reflect upon the remarkable escape from the Mound of Extremes where he would, without doubt, have perished had it not been for his friend.

There had been three black segments of the Source Disc yet to show above ground before the first lit segment would appear, and one-half of the first of these had moved on before Jed had managed to secure the second reflective dish firmly in place.

Brog, his eyesight impaired, had not held out

much hope of being able to cross to the Mountains of Separation before the Light came, but Jed had persuaded him it was worth the try.

The climb down the Mound had been the worst, but once on flat ground they began to make progress and, with a branch held between them so that Brog could be led, they had raced at top speed for the nearest tunnel entrance in the Mountains of Separation.

"Top speed" for Jed with his injury was not fast by any means, and they had been only about two-thirds of the way across the Valley when the first thin wafer of the first lit segment began to peep over the top of the plinth.

Brog had immediately sensed the change, and instinctively lengthened his stride, coming level with Jed.

"Run on, Brog! Run!" Jed had yelled, and Brog's burst of speed had left him gasping.

To Brog, the Mountains ahead had been a blur. He knew there was a tunnel entrance somewhere, but in his condition, it had been impossible to see it . . . until Jed had begun shouting directions, guiding him, sending him left when necessary, right, left again, keeping him on course for the entrance, aiming him like a throwstik to the target.

Those last few strides had been agony, the pain in the back of his head needle-sharp, as, screaming aloud with sheer determination, he had homed in on the entrance.

The dark mass had loomed large, filled what vision he had, as he had hurled himself into the cool depths of the tunnel, and crawled deeper into its welcoming recess.

Jed had joined him minutes later.

Two whole Dayspans they had lain inside the Mountain, fed and watered by the grateful Guardians, gathering their strength, luxuriating in the enormity of what they had accomplished, shuddering at the thought of how it *could* have turned out.

But their satisfaction was tinged with a bitter edge. Brog could never go back to his beloved Great Gloom.

The distance across the Glowurld was too great to be covered in one Blacktime.

With luck, and if they pushed themselves hard, they reckoned they would be able to reach the vicinity of the Glokeeper's castle, and so it was that, with Jed's leg rested and giving him less trouble, and Brog's eyes bruised but restored, they bade farewell to the Guardians and travelled throughout the following Black-time to where Brog now lay – in a darkened room of a dwelling set in a hollow, close by the castle so savagely brutalized by Redeye and his band.

The rebuilding of the castle was well under way, and though the people didn't know when a new Glokeeper might appear, Jed had already been asked to be his first assistant.

Brog had caused a stir amongst the Humans.

None of them had seen a Stoop before, and in the Blacktimes, when he was able to leave his room, they stared as he walked about with Jed.

Both were treated with great respect, and nothing was spared in an effort to make Brog feel at home.

"But this isn't home," he said now to Jed, as he nibbled the food he had brought. "And can never be, for me."

"I understand," muttered Jed.

"Do you?" said Brog. "To know that a few leagues away are your family, your friends . . . your true home? All of which you can never see again?"

"But Brog, I've told you, it can be arranged. If you will only let us help . . ."

"And I've told *you*, Jed, I won't be carried back to my homeland – in a cart!" and he spat the word out.

"Foolish pride. . . !" began Jed.

"Maybe so," cut in Brog, "but a Stoop *must* do all things with dignity, and of his own mettle, or not at all!"

"But, we can carry you in a darkened box to

within walking distance of the Great Gloom. No one need ever know."

"*I* would know!"

His manner softened, he scooped at the flesh of the segment of giant lushball he was pretending to eat.

"It must be difficult for you to understand, my friend, and it must appear that I'm ungrateful."

Jed shook his head. "No," he said. "Stubborn, but not ungrateful."

"I am a Stoop, Jed. Everything I do must be won, must be earned, must be . . . fought for. Every task I set myself must be accomplished, every problem solved. It is the way we are."

"But look at what you *have* accomplished," urged Jed. "Is that not enough?"

"But the task is not complete. Not until I return home under the conditions *I set myself!* . . . or . . ."

"Or. . . ?" Jed asked.

"Or until I die trying. To be carried even part of the way would be a betrayal of everything I am." He examined the thick rind of the lushball. "The Drabkeeper said to me: 'There is no danger that cannot be overcome by honesty.'" He looked at Jed. "I have to be honest with myself – true to my nature."

In the silence which followed, Jed eyed his friend sadly.

"You're going to try, aren't you – to get home?"

Brog flexed the rind, placed it around his eyes like a visor.

"Yes," he smiled, "I am."

CHAPTER 29

With great ceremony, they laid the body of Klan on an altar in the centre of the Flatplace, so that every Stoop from near and far could come and pay him their respects, give him their thanks for all he had done.

They laid him in the open where the precious Light for which he had fought could fall upon him, sending glints from his blond mane, reflecting from his polished battlewood and Ka'thuk, and even in death he looked magnificent.

It was agreed by all that he had been the greatest Stooplord the nation had ever known, and all mourned, not only for Klan, but for the loss of the only one who might have been able to fill his place – Brog, his son, to be known for ever more as Healer of the Light, who like his father, had given his life for the salvation of his people.

At the end of the first day of homage to Klan, as the Light was just beginning to gently fade, and the Flatplace was still crowded with mourners, an old, old Human in a pearl white robe walked from the trees and threaded his way through the crowd towards the altar which held Klan's body.

No one saw him, because no one *could* see him.

It was the spirit of the Glokeeper.

He reached the altar, and laid a hand on Klan's chest.

None of the watching Stoop, united in their grief, were able to see the spirit of Klan as it rose and stood by the body it no longer needed.

With a hand on the old man's shoulder, Klan walked slowly away from the altar, towards the tree-fringe, and there, waiting for him, her hood thrown back and a smile on her lips, was Blid.

The happiness on Klan's face matched her own, as she took his hand and led him away into eternity and a peace they could share for longer than time would exist.

*　　*　　*

The severed Gork hand, now withered and dry, lay in the ruins of the house exactly where Brog had last seen it. Jed kicked it aside with contempt as he and Brog entered after the long walk from the Glokeeper's castle.

There were still Blackhours left, but they could go no further. This was the nearest place of shelter to the Great Gloom. Ahead lay the unbroken Glowurld flatness which Brog had to attempt to cross within the space of the next Blacktime, but meanwhile there was a whole Dayspan to get through. The two friends set about building, amidst the ruin, a den in which Brog could rest away the Lighthours to come.

Long before the sky began to brighten, they had finished their task, and while Brog made himself comfortable inside, Jed went off to find a growplot which might provide sustenance for the two of them. He returned just as the Dayspan was beginning to find Brog safely enclosed, with all chinks in the stone-built hideaway filled with red clay.

They shared the food, and Jed sat up against the outside of the den, close to a gap in the wall farthest from the Source, where they could share a conversation. Both knew that the chances were slim for Brog to make the safety of the Treelands of the Great Gloom within the space of one Blacktime.

On his journey *into* the Glowurld, it had taken him a whole Span and half a Blacktime to get to this very point. True, he had only been travelling at an energy-saving lope, but he had been fresher then, and his eyesight had been better. This time, he would have to run more carefully to compensate for his impaired vision.

They talked until mid-span, not knowing when, or if, they would ever be able to talk again, and would have talked longer, but Jed insisted that Brog used the rest of the time to regenerate, in readiness for the journey. While Brog rested, Jed leaned against the den, keeping silent company with his friend.

It was not until the sky drew dim again that Brog emerged, anxious not to waste a moment of time, and it was because of this necessity to hurry, that their parting was mercifully brief. In the short time they had known each other they had shared great dangers, faced terrible odds, and formed a bond of trust between them that was as deep and as strong as any could be. This was probably the last time they would be together, and each was painfully aware of the fact. They embraced, twining arms around each other, then stood for a moment, building memories in their minds, taking one last look at a friend who might never be seen again.

"How will I know if you have reached home safely?" asked Jed.

Brog smiled. "Know that I have," he murmured, "For I will."

"Or die trying?" added Jed.

"To die trying is to die honestly," said Brog, "but fear not my friend, I will find a way to let you know, I promise."

"Go in peace then, Brog."

A final handclasp, then Brog turned and strode into the gathering darkness, and his blonde mane flew behind him as he broke into his run.

Urgency lent wings to his feet, and with his bruised eyes enlarged to their widest, he drove himself relentlessly towards his home.

At this pace, even he would eventually begin to tire, but he was hoping that, when he did, he would be near enough to be able to ease off and coast to safety. The important thing now was to cover as much distance as possible while the Blacktime was here.

There was utter silence save for the wind in his hair and the slap of his feet, and a million thoughts came to him of what he might find when he reached the Great Gloom – if he reached the Great Gloom . . .

He had covered maybe fifty leagues when he began to feel the effects of his punishing pace;

his legs were starting to feel heavy, and his breathing was becoming laboured. Another ten leagues and he was in trouble, sucking in air greedily through his nostrils. He knew he had to slow down, yet his instincts told him that the new Span was not far away. Relentlessly, he kept up the pressure and maintained his pace, though the effort, he knew, was killing him. But if that happened, he kept telling himself, then he would at least have died as a Stoop *should* die, striving for a goal.

He sensed, rather than saw, the lightening of the land ahead. The blackness before him eased into a shade of grey, which told him that the Dayspan was about to burst out. He had tried to outrun the Light, and had failed.

As the greyness gave way to hazier shades he stopped, opened the pouch around his waist, and brought out segments of moist lushball rind. These he laid, in triplicate, across his eyes, and bound them tightly with a rag.

The cool, soft flesh of the fruit eased the burning, and Brog smiled, but his smile was not due to any comfort or relief that the lushball rinds had brought him. A split-second before he had applied them to his eyes, he had seen, dimly, and in the distance, the outline of a tree-covered slope which could be only one thing . . . home.

In the Great Gloom, not everyone had mourned Brog.

There was one who refused to mourn him until the day that she could see and touch his dead body.

And so, each Blacktime, when the Light began to fade, Lin would stand atop the rock on the fringe of the Great Gloom, the same rock that she and Brog used to sit upon as Stooplings, and look out across the expanse of the Glowurld, waiting for her beloved Brog to come home.

Sometimes Pik and Kora would join her for a while, not to keep watch, but to give her company, knowing that sooner or later she would have to abandon her watch, accept her loss, grieve for Brog, and pick up the threads of her life.

It was on the third Blacktime of her watch that she noticed a large, red flower which seemed to have appeared since last she was there, and though there was no breeze, it was swaying backwards and forwards, its slender leaves, almost like arms, waving, and suddenly, for no reason she could explain, she no longer felt alone. It was almost as though the flower was watching with her.

Towards the end of that particular Blacktime, when Lin's senses told her that the new Dayspan was about to begin, but before the first streaks of Light had crept into the sky, a huge white bird flew in from the Uplands.

It swept down along the fringe of the Glo-wurld and headed out over the flatness to a point just within Lin's sight, where it began to circle round, each circuit bringing it lower.

And, as the sky began to lighten, and the whiteness of the bird took on a luminosity, she saw – or she thought she saw – that it was circling above a moving speck, but it could have been that her eyes were playing tricks.

A few strides from her, the red flower had begun to quiver violently, the 'arms' wrapping and unwrapping themselves around its stem, but Lin had no time to wonder at the pheno-menon, for now she was sure that the speck was moving, and it had become a figure!

Her heart leapt, excitement mingling with frustration, for very soon now the Light would become too strong for her to remain where she was and she would have to retreat into the Treelands.

She shaded her eyes, straining to see.

Out in the Glowurld, within sight of his homeland, but unable to see it, Brog staggered onward, the huge white bird that was the Drabkeeper circling above him, encouraging him, directing him, guiding him around the bloated bodies of the Gork scavengers killed by the restored Light six Dayspans ago, keeping him on a straight path that would bring him home.

As he stumbled along, the rays of the new Dayspan already beginning to ache his eyes, the first faint smell of the forest came to him.

"Drabkeeper," called Brog, "my friend Jed, the human . . ."

"Splendid young man, what of him?"

"Tell him I arrived safely, will you do that?"

"My pleasure," he quipped, "and now I must fly." He chuckled at the pun. "Straight on, Brog, straight on, not too far now."

His voice began to get fainter as he widened the circle he was flying.

"Listen, call round and see me sometime, you know where I live . . . bring that little friend of yours, whatsisname. . .?"

"Planimal," said Brog.

"Planimal, of course . . . and that pretty young thing who's waiting for you, bring her too."

Brog's heart leaped. "Lin?"

"That her name?"

"Lin? She's alive? Lin is alive?"

"Alive and waiting, young Brog."

Brog's smile was so wide it puckered the sore skin around his eyes, but he didn't feel the pain.

The one thing he had been dreading since his ordeal had ended, the one thing he hadn't dared to hope was that Lin might have survived. Now he knew she had, nothing else mattered.

"Some people get all the luck," quipped the Drabkeeper.

With a flap of his great wings he wheeled away, and Brog heard his voice fading into the distance, shouting his final instructions:

"Straight on, Brog . . . straight on . . . straight onnnnn . . ."

And then silence but for the sound of his own feet shuffling over the hard-baked surface.

Lin trembled with excitement in the bush just inside the Great Gloom.

Through the dappled branches she peered as closely as she dared, eyes slitted, into the white haze that the Glowurld had become in the short space of time since the Dayspan had broken.

She saw nothing, could see nothing, but still she stared, knowing that Brog, if it was he, must be near to the fringe, would need the assistance she so desperately wanted to give him. Doubts began to assail her mind. Had she really seen anything? Had she seen only what she had wanted to see? A shadow crossed her vision, bobbing, swaying, became darker, more bulky, she heard the crunch of leaves underfoot, the snap of a branch, the slap of a welcoming hand on a trunk, Brog's huge sigh of relief . . . and a strange, high-pitched, piping chuckle.

"Brog!" she called, unable to keep the tremble from her voice.

The shadow stiffened, the head bobbed, searching for direction.

"Brog!"

He tore the cover from his eyes. "Lin? Is that you?"

Then, suddenly he was striding towards her, becoming clearer with each step.

With amazement, Lin saw that sitting on his shoulder was a strangely familiar creature, a smile written across its red face, clapping its thin, green hands in delight.

The creature jumped down and danced delightedly around them as Brog crushed Lin to him in an embrace.

He held her there for an age, unable to believe he was doing so, unable to believe he was home, until finally, she took his hand and led him off through the cool, leafy Gloom to the future he had made possible for all who lived there, the future he would share with Lin for as long as he lived.

EPILOGUE

In a black, forgotten corner of the Darkness lay an egg, carried there by a now-dead Gork, the only egg ever to have been found in the search when the Stoop had raided the Nesting Stations.

The egg which Pik had used as bait.

The crack in its shell split and widened, and out into that utter Blackness crawled a Gorkling whose eyes burned red.

Joe Boyle

JOE BOYLE was born in Fleetwood, Lancashire, and now lives with his wife, Lesley, in Birkenhead. He has two daughters, Lisa and Heidi, and a grand-daughter, Sophie aged eighteen months.

Although he left teaching to become a full-time writer, he still retains an interest in the teaching of Art, and has a love of poetry.

Much of his writing is for television with episodes of *Emmerdale* and *Brookside* to his credit, and his situation comedy *HELP!* of recent years, achieved audience ratings of around ten million.

He now writes for children of all ages, and enjoys the task of stimulating both humour and imagination in his readers.